Patrice Chaplin, noveor
of fourteen works o   g
(Virago 1992), Siesta   t.
Her first stage play *From the Balcony* was performed at
the National Theatre and in various capitals around the
world. Her second, *Ruby in the Dust*, opened in London
in spring 1992. She is currently writing the stage play of
*Into the Darkness Laughing: The Story of Jeanne Hébuterne,
Modigliani's Last Mistress* (Virago 1990).

By the same author

Fiction
A Lonely Diet
The Last of the Big Kite Flyers
Cry Wolf
By Flower and Dean Street
Siesta
The Unforgotten
Don Salino's Wife
The Fame People
Forget-Me-Not
Saraband
Harriet Hunter
Night Fishing
Albany Park

Non-fiction
Into the Darkness Laughing: The Story of Jeanne Hébuterne,
Modigliani's Last Mistress
Another City

Having It Away

PATRICE CHAPLIN

Published by VIRAGO PRESS Limited 1993
20–23 Mandela Street, Camden Town, London NW1 0HQ

Copyright © Patrice Chaplin 1977

First published in Britain by Gerald Duckworth & Co. Ltd. 1977

A CIP catalogue record for this book is available from the British Library

Printed and bound in Great Britain by
Cox & Wyman Ltd, Reading, Berkshire

I

James was standing by the phone when Charmian called, but then Charmian always chose the most inconvenient moment for everything.

It was impossible, without making James suspicious, for Jenny to answer any of her questions, all of them about Luis – Would he be there? Was he still as beautiful – as sexy? Was Jenny looking forward to him? James was alerted, though, by her non-committal answers. As he reached for a book he came nearer the phone, and he could hardly miss Charmian's 'What will you do about James? We don't want an acrimonious scene.'

'Hello! Hello!' Pretending she'd been cut off, Jenny hung up. The silence that followed was nasty and she escaped into the chaos of packing.

'Why are you taking that?' he asked, eyeing a new white evening dress. 'You won't need that. Why are you taking all that perfume? I thought the place was supposed to be deserted.'

'Just because there's no one about doesn't mean I have to look a mess, does it?'

'Perhaps I will come out there now,' he said softly. 'I can finish my work when I get back.'

'As you like.' She'd have to spend the rest of the evening delicately persuading him to keep to their first

5

arrangement, the one where she had two weeks without him, two weeks during which she could be with Luis, her Spanish lover.

The flat was mournful in the summer light. Winter greys, wet greys suited it. They soothed its gloom. Sun brought out the dust, the low ceilings, the muddle, the cumbersome cupboards.

'What a dump,' she heard him say. 'Why should I stick in such a dump?'

Sharp retorts came effortlessly. She resisted them. Why not leave on a good note?

They didn't have much to say to each other, but then they never had. Lately all the things that had made their affair worthwhile seemed to have gone out of it. James was torn between uncomfortable security with her and dubious freedom. It didn't mean he wasn't jealous, though.

She couldn't find the tickets. Her younger son Francis remembered putting them behind the clock.

'But we haven't got a clock!' she said.

'He means the gas meter, Mum,' said Tom, the elder boy.

'Why? In God's name, why?'

'I don't think he wants to go, Mum.'

She couldn't get all the clothes in one case and had to rely on too many carrier bags – paper ones – that would be dissolved by squashed food in damp boats.

'Why d'you need all that?' asked James querulously. 'Why d'you need your winter coat? You are coming back, aren't you?'

She'd go over to the pub, put down enough drink so

she didn't care, then pack again, ruthlessly, just the stuff she'd need for six weeks in the sun.

The phone rang and Charmian said, 'The arrangements will have to be changed. Laurence has decided to come to the station to see me off. So, Jenny, get to the station half an hour after me. Don't let Laurence see you, whatever happens. Get in the first carriage. Then when the train starts you can move up to where we are. No slip-ups at this stage, please,' she ordered.

'But what about Norman?' Norman was Charmian's lover.

'Well, he could do the same as you and keep out of sight. But, over-cautious as usual, he's decided to get another train altogether. It means he'll have to get up before 6 a.m. and wait for hours at Folkestone.' She laughed loudly. 'Another thing. Don't mention Norman in front of Adam, whatever you do. He mustn't know he's coming, in case he says something to Laurence.'

Adam, 5, was her eldest child. Sophie, 4, had a natural discretion about her mother's affairs. Little Peter, 2, could speak but couldn't understand – she hoped.

'What will Adam think when Norman joins us on the boat?' There was a long pause. 'Are you still there?' Jenny could hear her dragging heavily on a cigarette.

'I don't know. Anyway, it will be too late for him to say anything to Laurence then, won't it?'

'What will Laurence think if the train's crowded and you're surrounded by reserved seats, all empty? Won't he get the feel of a party with half its members not turned up? Very suspicious. Surely it would be better for Laurence not to come to the station at all but

7

to say goodbye at the flat.' She wasn't looking forward to lugging cases and kids through the train when it was moving. 'Then we can all travel together peacefully.'

'You don't know Laurence. He'll insist. He's that sort of man. He likes seeing people off from stations, choosing seats, buying magazines. He sends people flowers. That's Laurence. He'll insist, all right. Don't forget, he doesn't want me to go. After all, he loves me.'

Norman must be in the background, suffering.

Another thrust. 'He's begged me not to go, Jenny.'

'Norman was definitely there. She wouldn't waste it on a woman. Another cigarette being lit.

'Christ I must give up smoking. It's killing me. But my nerves are shreds. I can't wait to get away. I must have peace. I need peace. Don't forget your passport. We don't want any mishaps.'

While making the breakfast, Jenny wrote soothing notes to tradesmen delaying yet again outstanding accounts. She powdered her face. She was exhausted. She'd spent half the night making love to James. He still wasn't cheered up.

'Finish your work, James. Then come out. Of course it makes sense. You won't have it hanging over you then.' She sighed. He was studying for a PhD, had been for years, but the cold fact of his thirtieth birthday in a few months caused him to fear for his future. There weren't as many jobs for lecturers as there used to be. The thought of teaching foreign businessmen basic grammar for the rest of his life made him suicidal.

The eggs were burning.

Tom had diarrhoea, travel nerves.

The case still wouldn't do up.

'I haven't a hope of getting the train. I'm not even dressed.'

The phone rang. Charmian said, 'The arrangements will have to be changed again. Get to the station half an hour before me and go to the far end of the train, right out of the way. Otherwise, when the train goes out, Laurence standing on the platform, waving, might spot you.'

'Impossible! I'm late as it is.'

'Oh, all right. But stick to last night's plan and be careful, or the whole holiday could be ruined.'

Jenny could hear Charmian's au paur savaging the unruly children with combs and face flannels, turning them into something halfway acceptable for foreign lands. Charmian, it seemed, was still in bed.

'I've got a bit of a hangover. That's another thing I've got to give up, Jenny.'

They were going to Spain because they needed tranquillity and sun. Laurence might have needed it too, but he was staying in England. Not that he'd had any choice. Charmian told him her nerves were bad. She needed to look at sunsets, deserted beaches, earthy peasant life. It seemed she could only look at things on her own.

The morning was scorching and there was the usual traffic confusion in the Finchley Road. There were several free taxis at ten, but Jenny would have got there too soon. When she wanted one there weren't any.

James, who was helping get the luggage to the station, jumped up and down with rage.

'She's doing this to bugger everybody about as usual. Why should I be put through all this just to shield Laurence from the truth of her holiday? If she's so clever that she can get him to believe she's going to Spain on her own for six weeks, why can't she do a simple thing like stop him coming to the station? You're going to miss the train.'

By the time they'd got to the train, James seemed relieved he wasn't coming. Sweating, he put the cases into the first carriage. Jenny hissed at Francis to keep out of sight.

Four minutes to go.

'Go and see where our carriage is, James. I'll move up near it. I'll never manage all this on my own.'

It was a relief-train and surprisingly empty. There were hardly any people on the platform. No sign of Laurence saying a sad farewell to his wife. No sign of his wife, either.

The reserved compartment was in Coach B1.

'There's no B1 and no Charmian,' said James, coming back. He looked pasty.

Two minutes to go.

'Don't say Laurence has found out about Norman?' Should she phone Charmian?

She got off the train. Then she thought of Norman stranded at Folkestone.

The guard started closing doors.

'She's coming now,' said James.

'Is Laurence with her?' Jenny got out of sight.

'No.'

She was pushing a trolley piled with children and luggage.

'Where's the compartment?' she asked, panting.

'Get in here,' said James savagely. 'We're not moving again.'

'I couldn't get a taxi. Phoned for nearly an hour. In the end Laurence rode up and down on his bicycle looking for one.'

'Where is he?' asked James.

'Back at the flat. Absolutely worn out.'

James looked at the ground.

'And then I went to the wrong train.'

The whistle blew.

'You'd better get in,' he said. 'Or you'll miss it altogether. Goodbye.' He tried to kiss Jenny, but Charmian, cases and kids were in the way.

'When are you coming out, James?' Charmian asked, as though she didn't know.

'In two weeks.' Then he looked at her. He either fancied her or hated her. Most men felt that about Charmian at some time or other.

'Why don't you come with us now?' She winked at Jenny. 'Come on. I bet you've got your passport.' She seemed to be inviting him to more than a trainride.

He blushed. 'Well, I have actually.''

Jenny turned pale and kicked Charmian, who laughed uproariously. The train started before he could make up his mind.

This holiday was my idea. The phrase seemed to settle into Jenny's mind. It made her feel cold.

II

As she came up the stairs on to the top deck, the first thing Jenny saw were Norman's feet. His shoes were small, pointed and very clean. In front of them was Charmian's pushchair, its wheels clogged with the dried stodge of dropped sweets and ice cream; behind them stood his heavy case. He was all surrounded by the responsibilities of the holiday; yet his feet looked detached and swift as though they could make a quick getaway if they had to. When she shouted 'Norman', the feet sped off. She ran on to the deck.

'Hullo, Jenny,' he said faintly and disappeared behind the mast.

Charmian and Jenny rounded up the flock of children to the middle of a deck and tried to keep them there.

'I wish to God Norman would hurry up and find us,' said Charmian. 'What the hell is he doing?'

'I've just seen him. He ran away.'

'What's the matter with him, for crissake? No, Little Peter, not near the rails. Come back, Adam! Adam!' she screamed. 'You're not to put your head through. Because you'll fall in. It does make sense. Don't climb up. No, not down the stairs. Christ! Perhaps, Jenny, it's a good thing we didn't get the travel insurance. Imagine the relief of losing one of these and getting a thousand quid as well.'

'I want an ice cream,' said Adam.

'Don't dare say that word,' she whispered, savagely, but Little Peter had heard it.

'Ice cream. Now!'

'Now look what you've done, Adam!'

'An orange squash then,' said Adam, reasonably.

'No!' she shrieked.

'Squash! Squash!' said Little Peter, clawing at her.

'Where the hell's Norman?' asked Charmian.

'He's probably scared that Laurence has made an unexpected dash to keep his marriage going and is here on the boat.'

Jenny's children were creeping away across a forbidden area looped off with ropes. Tom was 4, had little sense, but could be persuaded to do what he was told. Francis was 3, had plenty of sense and did the opposite of what he was told. There was a short scrappy row, at the end of which they were sitting with the others on a long seat.

The sun blazed, the sea was heavy and full, its waves barely lapping, one after the other against the boat. Gulls screeched after the food tipped out from the galley. Halfway across the Channel they flew back and were replaced by French gulls, cawing, screeching out from the shore. The boat cut through the water, making a white angry froth.

A sailor looked at the five children, momentarily quiet, and said, 'You'll have to move them from here.' He pointed at the funnel. 'When that goes off the blast will give them a terrible fright.'

'I doubt it,' said Charmian.

'Take them to the end of the boat,' he said.

'All I want,' she said to Jenny, as she dragged herself up, 'is peace. I need peace desperately.'

About the time the English gulls flew back, Norman appeared beside them and for Adam's benefit did a scene of wild surprise. It was quite wasted. Charmian had talked about Norman non-stop, and by now Adam must have known that Norman was coming with them. He didn't say anything – but then, when his father wasn't with his mother Norman was.

Charmian's face was pale and strained. At Folkestone she'd had two complications with her passport. First, she'd written in the names of her children herself. Not allowed. Little Peter didn't appear in the passport at all. Secondly, the passport was out of date.

'Three months,' said the official.

'Oh God. I can't go back now.'

She refused to move. She lit a cigarette and took her time doing it.

The queue sighed.

Then the official looked at Charmian, at her eyes, at her body – especially at her body. 'I'll let you through,' he said, 'but I don't think you'll get into France.'

'What will happen?'

'You'll be sent back on the next boat.'

She allowed Norman two minutes of happy holiday anticipation and then showed him the passport. His face sagged, became all chin like a hippopotamus's. How-

14

ever, he hid his displeasure under a surface of extreme reasonableness. As Charmian powdered her face with a huge pink puff, he outlined a reasonable plan.

'We'll all go through the passport control together. We'll have a porter for the luggage. I'll create a bit of a diversion and they may not notice you. If they don't let you through, Jenny will get the train with her children and luggage and we'll go to the Consul in Boulogne and get the passport renewed. Jenny will go on to Spain and we'll follow.' He puffed on his pipe, desperately.

'Norman's got it all worked out, Jenny. I don't know what I'd do without him.' She smiled provocatively.

Norman was small, only a little bit taller than Charmian. He had dark, sensitive eyes that tried to hide in the impassivity of his face, which was pale and careful. His yellow powdery hair was combed into his idea of how it should look – it fell immediately into unstartling disarray. His mouth was non-committal, his hands delicate.

Because of the five whining children, sprawling luggage and no man (Norman was in the bar getting Charmian a large drink), a sailor showed the women the best place on the boat to wait to get off first. Jenny supposed the favour had something to do with Charmian's breasts. Sometimes she seemed to have all her vitality concentrated inside them.

Charmian had a plump sexy body with long rounded thighs in dark brown nylon stockings. Above the rich body, her face, a pale oval, was smooth and serene; her blue eyes were long-lashed, quick and intelligent.

15

Her hair, soft and fluffy, was always full of the whims of some hairdresser; coloured and cudgelled and bounced, and costing ten pounds a week, it still managed to look like hair. She survived. A bottle of red wine and half a bottle of whisky a night and her liver might be quivering, but she was always there in the morning, with the pram-load of kids, doing her shapely struggle up the hill to the nursery. Her voice was light and quick, and she always said precisely what she meant to say. Laurence was a scientist, and she an unwilling housewife with a degree in history of art.

Norman's plan for going through the passport control might possibly have worked if they'd all got off the boat together. But Charmian unaccountably disappeared before it docked. She was in the bar and because of the huge thick queue winding through the decks couldn't get back to them again.

Children and cases were dotted about Boulogne station. Sophie was hysterical. Norman felt desperately in need of his pipe, realised it was already in his mouth and pawed his pockets for a tranquillizer.

Charmian was eventually wound round in the last curl of the queue. There was a choice of uniformed men, and she hesitated. The one she chose stared at the passport officiously, turned the pages quickly. His passport-examining glare was good and had them all terrified, but he didn't notice the date.

Paris-Austerlitz station – cut-throat atmosphere choking with queues, noise, sweat, jostling. An American boy asked a porter where the train for Rome was. The porter, as usual, made no effort to understand an

16

attempt at French and shuffled off with a huffy 'Comprends pas'.

The boy was distraught. His ticket expired at midnight and he'd spent the whole afternoon going from station to station trying to find the train. 'They just don't care.'

At the door of the restaurant, the manager was bloated with bad temper, his own food and general frogginess. No, he did not have a table for five children under five and three people around thirty.

'Will there be one?' asked Norman, all politeness and reason.

'*Non.*'

They hovered by the door. The train left in forty minutes. People stared. Who was who in their group? They were sorting that out a lot of the time too. The restaurant was packed. Norman's shoes were looking black and gleaming. Thinking of escape? A porter had tried to charge him one franc a case for moving them a few yards to the Left Luggage, and Norman had told him to stuff it.

'The next time I come to France will be at the head of an invading army. I'll carry them to the train myself.'

'Oh forget it,' said Charmian, irritably. 'Pay.'

Charmian and Jenny stood in the middle of the station while Norman struggled to the couchette compartment with all the luggage.

'Shall we help him?' Jenny asked.

Charmian didn't know. There was a definite lack of system. She put on her dark glasses and had that *je-ne-*

sais-exactement-quoi expression. It got the men at it. A Frenchman was staring at her.

'How do I look?' she asked Jenny.

The Frenchman approached, and Jenny watched Norman saving one franc pieces and building up for a hernia.

'Shall I go and get some food?' said Jenny.

'No. We'll sort it out in a minute.' She was staring at the Frenchman.

'Where are you from?' he started to ask but couldn't take his eyes off her legs.

She removed her glasses and told him her name.

Charmian cared what men thought of her, needed them to think of her. 'She's after everyone's man so I have to have her as my best friend,' Jenny had moaned more than once.

Charmian told the man something about London, after which she moved her tongue along her top lip slowly. His body was blazing.

Norman, from a distance, assessed the scene correctly and rushed over. Charmian looked at the Frenchman and took her time saying goodbye. A smile Norman couldn't miss. More fuel to keep the pot aboil.

'Come on,' he said roughly. His life was always strewn with rivals.

The children wouldn't sleep. Little Peter was allowed to bugger about. Charmian had one rule for the other kids and another for him. He could do what he liked. He was strong, wild, passionate; he ate dirt, crapped his pants and, like a dog, peed everywhere as though marking the territory. Little Peter bit people, spoke as little as he could and yowled a lot. He had angelic features and white hair.

At midnight Little Peter tottered along the corridor with his bottle hanging by its teat from between his teeth. He bent to eat a cigarette end.

Norman said, 'He's primitive.'

'Prehistoric,' said Charmian. 'He's giving these frogs something to think about. They're *bourgeois*.' 'Bourgeois', when expletives weren't enough, was her ultimate insult.

Charmian seemed surprised when the other children, jealous of the attention Little Peter was getting, wouldn't stay in their beds. Jenny said they should *all* be up, or none of them. Little Peter, after howling like a wolf, was flattened across his bed and finally sank into a snoozling sleep, teat flubbering against his lips. 'He's so sensual,' Charmian whispered.

Norman's paintings were considered calm. Looking at them, however, Jenny always felt disturbed. Norman painted scenery, never people. Jenny thought that was because he didn't like them enough to paint them. He'd been to public school and Oxford and had a detached personality. No one knew what he was thinking, much less feeling. His response to people came from a foot away from him. He was inside, looking, thinking about something else altogether.

Charmian said his old man had money and so, she suspected, had Norman. Perhaps it was Charmian's spending habits (she had got through £16,000 of Laurence's in three years) that made Norman keep it –

19

if he had it – out of sight. He told her he supported himself by his painting.

Norman and Charmian spent most of their time alone in her flat listening to music and making love. They brought out in each other qualities that couldn't exist with anyone else. The only obstacle, it seemed, was Laurence. Laurence came home every weekend and she didn't see Norman then. It had worked out – for the first six months she'd been happy. 'I could get the best from both of them, but now I can't keep them separate any more. What I feel for Norman is spilling into my marriage. I can't let Laurence make love to me anymore.' Laurence, tormented, frustrated, was getting violent. The time was right for Charmian to give up her marriage and go and live with Norman. Norman, however, seemed a little reticent about suggesting it.

It was possibly two a.m. and the wine was finished long ago. 'Are you looking forward to seeing Luis?' Charmian asked Jenny.

'I don't know.'

'If you're with Luis, what will you do about James?'

'I don't know.'

'You'll have to decide.'

'While we're being so concerned with choice, what are you going to do about Laurence? When you get back he'll know Norman's been with you. Adam will tell him.'

'I know. Of course I know.'

'What did you tell Laurence about this holiday? Won't he expect to come and see you?'

'I told him I needed to get away and be on my own.

20

He said, "All right, as long as there's no man involved".'

Norman came and stood beside them in the corridor and she said, loudly, 'But Laurence knows a man's in it somewhere. He knows me.'

Norman didn't wince.

Maybe he winced inside.

'You'll choose Luis in the end, though. I know you,' said Charmian.

'Not necessarily.'

Charmian looked at her. 'It's Charmian you're talking to.' A pause. 'He's attractive, James. But I don't like him. He doesn't like me either.'

'James is too down. Life gets him down, kids get him down,' said Norman. 'Domesticity obviously isn't for him, yet he sticks in it. I think he's masochistic.'

'I'm not very happy,' Jenny admitted.

'So you're escaping,' said Charmian.

'What's wrong with that?'

Jenny watched the black trees grizzling and gnarled against the sky, a clear sky with a huge moon: France, heavy and sensuous with summer, its hills soft and shivery with moonlight. The train rushed through the night, clattered through like a monster with many yellow eyes. She'd been in love with Luis since she was sixteen and although she'd been married, had lovers, she couldn't stop wanting him. Elusive, changeable, he was always just out of reach.

She went into the compartment and lay down.

They were somewhere near the roof making love. A piece of clothing floated down past her head. She'd

21

never heard people making love before and was surprised to find that she felt excluded. The sound, though, was fascinating.

'I couldn't do it if other people were there, especially children. Christ! I'm beginning to think like James.'

She'd known James for a year. He'd insisted she drop the domestic anarchy – the kind that flourished at Charmian's place – and restore order and discipline. He couldn't take a domestic scene at the best of times, so the one he was in had to be good. Not being a fool, he didn't give her any choice. If order and discipline weren't there he wouldn't be either.

Afterwards Norman swung about like an ape. Sexual pride? Only trying to find an empty bunk. Silence.

Charmian whispered, 'Norman, I can't find my bra.'

'It must have fallen down,' he said sleepily.

'Where?'

'I don't know.'

'Have a look will you?'

'In the morning.'

So they were going to Spain for six weeks. They were going for tranquility and sun.

'Where's my bra, Norman?'

Norman, at the same time as opening a bottle of water for the kids, searched briefly among the tangle of blankets.

'I can't see it, sweetie.'

'It must be there.'

'Well, I can't see it.'

'Can *you*, Jenny?'

'Come down and look.'

'I'm not coming down till I've got it on.'

Norman sighing? Only drawing on his pipe.

Breakfast trolley, ringing. 'I'll get it,' Jenny said.

'No, I will,' said Norman. They were still at the stage of being careful with each other, of not pushing or dominating or thinking of shares or rights – only the well-being of the group mattered. She covered her exhaustion with make-up.

'Is it under the beds?' asked Charmian.

'No,' said Norman.

'Give me a cigarette.'

'You'd better get up. We'll be there in half an hour.'

'Well, let's get there then. I'm not getting up without it.'

'Doe doe. Doe doe.' Little Peter clawed at Norman and Norman searched the floor for his bottle. 'There's no water left, Little Peter. I'll go and get you some juice.' He went out after the trolley.

Charmian was grinning like a Cheshire cat. 'He made love to me half the night. I'm absolutely exhausted now, but I can't do without my pleasures. Norman! Norman! The only thing to do is to get me another one.'

She slid the door open. He wasn't getting the juice after all. He was hiding in the corridor.

'Where is another one, Charmian?' He sighed and lit his pipe again. Smoke billowed up. A peace offering?

'In the case at the end of the corridor.'

23

The carriage had disintegrated. The floor was soggy – pieces of food floated in the deeper puddles. Blankets hung down. One assumed the liquid was spilt juice. The ticket collector looked baffled.

Norman was bent over the huge case searching forlornly through layer after layer of clothes.

'Ask Charmian exactly where it is.'

'Where is it?'

'In the case, for godsake!'

Norman shut it with a snap and silently stood in the corridor looking at passing France like any other man beginning a holiday. The racket in the compartment and Charmian's unsupported breasts no longer concerned him. She was obliged to put on her coat and go and find a bra herself. The other one turned up, floral and suggestive, from among the tufts of Little Peter's disposable napkins.

The queue was immense at Port Bou. It jolted forward, anaemic, tired, tickets in its mouths, awkward with cases.

They sat and waited till the end.

A Guardia Civil officer looked at the abundance of kids, Charmian and Jenny, and whistled at Norman appreciatively.

'Which one's your wife?'

Norman coughed.

The officer pointed at Jenny.

'No.'

'Her?' – meaning Charmian.

'No.'

'Neither your wife. But they're all your children?'

'No.'

'Which ones are your children?'

'None of them.'

He was amazed. 'None of them belongs to you? Then what are you doing here?'

III

Jenny wouldn't have gone near Gerona, but Norman insisted that that was where they got off. Jenny knew it should be Flassa, three stops north; but Norman preferred to trust a gaudy travel brochure.

Luis lived in Gerona. Jenny was going to San Pedro Pescador, and in two weeks James would arrive. They'd have a holiday and all go back together at the end of August. Her life, in the light of the morning's hangover, was a decisive thing. Luis was going to be nowhere near it.

The sky was grey and the train took an age going a few kilometres. They were grotesquely tired. Norman kept saying, 'We've got six weeks to get over it. I can't believe I'm here.' Jenny believed him.

Gerona – its old part riddled with magnificent churches, courtyards, Arab baths, narrow streets, ancient stairways, tunnels. Put off by the new part of town, the tourists left it alone and veered off to the coast. The cathedral, catching all the light of the early sun, seemed to hang over the town. It stuck up, hung down, massively.

'Twelfth-century,' said Norman suddenly.

'Please don't start on that,' Charmian snapped. 'I'm

here to see people, not read guide books. He reduces everything,' she said to Jenny.

He mumbled something about Charlemagne.

Mishearing the name, she thought he was insulting her and kicked him. 'My head aches. How it aches.'

Gerona, and the sun was brilliant.

The taxi went through the old part, close to the Ramblas. Behind them, in an alley, was Montserrat's shop; inside it, Luis. Jenny jumped out and, with heart pounding, hurried along the cobbled street. Gerona had a heady, intoxicating atmosphere, full of scent, olive oil and harsh tobacco. Motor bikes rattled past, the noise spitting like gunfire among the low stone arches of the Ramblas.

The shop was full of *objets d'art*, paintings, lamps. .Jenny saw Montserrat among the chinkeries and shadows. Montserrat saw her. Montserrat looked as though she wanted to run away, but Jenny pinned her with her stare, opened the door, gave her a smile and said, 'Ola.'

Montserrat said 'Ola', and the bottom dropped out of her life. The English girl was back.

'Luis?'

'Not here.' She fluttered against the wall like a stuck moth.

'Where?'

'I don't know. Not in Gerona any more.' Her face was pinched. She was wearing her painter's smock. Two of her water colours stood on easels by the door. They had surprising price tags on them. Jenny supposed Luis was responsible for that – he was always

27

optimistic about other people's money. Art was the thing in Gerona. Every other middle-class person was an 'artist'. The richer ones had exhibitions. Arty women clung together in cafés and talked about 'movements'.

'Adios,' said Jenny.

'Adios.' Montserrat hugged the till, as though by holding on to it she'd hold on to him.

Jenny crossed the alley and went into Antonio's shop. Yes, Luis was in Gerona sometimes. At others? Who knows where he is?

'He's not married?' she asked.

'Who to? Montserrat? She would like, yes. But Montserrat, although she is rich, makes one peseta go a long way. Luis, he doesn't like that.'

'Tell him I'm staying in San Pedro Pescador. Tell him to come and see me.'

He would. If he saw him.

Outside Gerona the sun disappeared. It always felt as though it was shining in Gerona, even when it wasn't.

Luis woke up. The sun pierced the cracks and gaps in the shutters – long, spiky pieces of sun like brilliant straw. A heavy fly whirred up and down the blue white walls. The cathedral bell was tolling; the huge sound rolled through the stone houses. Conversations stopped. The sound was echoed by lesser churches across the river. He could hear the raucous gossip of the old women as they shuffled up the cobbled street carrying bundles of washing to scrub at the stream. Wednesday morning. He looked at his watch. Five to ten.

He turned over and went back to sleep.

When he woke again, the Coca-Cola lorry was shuddering outside Pedro's bar. The noise was trapped in the narrow street, held down by the foggy heat.

The sun had gone in, the fly was silent. He heard his mother going slowly down the steps, her breath noisy and insufficient. Surprisingly, the upward journey was always quiet. She went next door to the milk shop for a litre of Leche Ram. He'd prefer tinned Nestles, if he could afford it. It was after eleven, and he felt luxuriously rested. Whistling, he got out of bed and looked at the paintings by the door. They always gave him pleasure. He opened the shutters and the hundred caged birds on the balconies above the street chirped loudly. His balcony was full of climbing plants and pots of scarlet flowers. A sudden heavy feeling took all joy out of the day. Was it because of Montserrat? The threat of marriage to Montserrat was not doing him any good. He could hear his mother in the cleaners asking for his trousers.

'How is your son?' asked the assistant.

'Marvellous.'

'He always looks so young.'

'He is young.'

Silence, as the woman remembered the 'thirties. Her recollection of his birth was hazy, but it had certainly happened before the war.

'Is he going to marry Montserrat Garcia Ortega?'

'Nothing is settled,' his mother snapped. Mention of that name could do her in for the day.

Then he heard her launch their latest rumour. He

29

had been offered a big job in Paris. Only people who didn't know him would believe it.

Sighing, he bent and did up his shoes. He could feel the lovely cold coming up off the stone floor. It glistened on the white walls, the sheets. Gerona in mid-July had few cool places.

His dog followed him into the tiny water closet. It followed him everywhere. The pile of newspaper by the pan was replaced by an unwrapped roll of pink lavatory paper – so a guest was expected. As he brushed his hair he thought suddenly of Jenny. He did up his belt. His waistline was soft – as a result, undeniably, of years of neglect, years of knowing that women found him attractive. For over twenty years that had been enough.

He ate the tortilla quickly and complained about the milk. 'Get Nestles, for godsake. They're putting powder in the bottled milk to make it whiter. This country is shit. There'll be a scandal, you'll see.'

He spread two biscuits with the last of the old tin of Nestles and ate them ravenously. Sleep always gave him an appetite.

'Why do you hang my trousers like that?' he said. 'They'll be all creased. D'you want me to look like an English tourist?'

His mother, ironing his shirt, didn't answer.

'Dampen it more. And try and disguise the cuffs. They're frayed.'

'Ugly twisted bitch,' she muttered. 'Thinks she can buy the whole world. Even my son. She'll never give you children. Impossible with a body like that.'

'Montserrat's all right. She can give birth.'

'Yes. To a monster.'

Clang of doorbell and a young man asked if he should start hanging the portraits for the competition in the Town Hall.

'I run this town,' said Luis, when he'd gone. 'I do everything. It's me who organises the fiestas. I do the flower display in the church, to which thousands come – last year over fifteen thousand. It's shown on the television. Yet what do they pay me? I don't even have the money to use a public lavatory.'

'You should have married that Austrian. She was lousy with money.'

'She killed herself.'

'You should have stopped her. This fiancée's no good. Too acid. The only fat on her is round her ankles.'

'That's because of her heart trouble. Her legs are much better since I made her have the operation.'

'She looks bad-tempered, as though her shoes pinch. And she'll hang on to her money. You've run round her for over a year. Where does it get you? You're forty-five.'

'Forty-three.'

'I should know. You haven't got a peseta.'

'When I win the fat one, my life will change.'

The 'fat' lottery was drawn once a year. They also had the 'tourist' lottery. His sister gave him the money for the tickets.

The garden was a fenced-off bit of the mountain, sloping up to the house and rising steeply behind it. In front, it was all short grass and flowers; at the back, tall trees, thick shrubbery and nervous snakes. Last-minute preparations were still happening, in true Spanish style. Workmen were laying a new cement terrace and the door was being screwed on. At least there was a roof, and for that they should be grateful. The house was outside the village. It had this large garden, completely fenced in, no neighbours. Its furniture was plain and functional, the decor simple, and it didn't look as though it needed protecting. On the face of it, it seemed a good place for the children.

The owner's wife came round the side of the house, all *nouveau riche* and outrage. Her eyes sparked on when she saw Charmian, and even at that distance Jenny could see that it was hate at first sight. Charmian, in her see-through blouse, was not quite what the woman had had in mind as a tenant.

The man from the agency, sensing a discomfort in his client, said a quick Buenas and being no fool got into his car and fled.

Norman walked up the steps to the woman, revealed that he could speak Spanish and rescued the situation.

Meanwhile Little Peter had toddled off round the back of the house and found an outside tap. He was thrilled, as the water splashed on to the concrete.

The woman did a dance and grabbed Norman.

Norman told Charmian to smack him.

Charmian sank into a chair near the terrace and said, 'I hope we have better weather than this, Jenny. It's colder than London.'

The woman would have a word with the man in the agency about Little Peter.

The kids, with all the garden available, had to confine themselves to the space around the gate. They were already bored and trying to get out. The cement terrace now had the appearance of well-trodden snow.

'Come in,' said Norman. 'She wants to explain the house to you.'

'No,' said Charmian. 'There've been several Señoras like her in my life and it's always ended badly. You get on with it, Norman.'

Below them, three roads met at the gate and swept away again. One trailed out of the village, limping with carts, workmen and dogs, another, white and professional, held the holiday traffic avoiding San Pedro Pescador and whizzing down the Costa Brava; and the last, lined at the beginning with a few houses, stretched almost to the gate, and then zinged back, circling, curving up into the hills.

'I can see Laurence coming along one, James along the other, and Norman and Luis escaping along the third,' said Jenny.

'Don't even joke about it.' Charmian was shocked. 'Thank God it's a good look-out point.'

The air made them sleepy, agitated and extremely hungry all at once, and didn't suit Charmian right from the start. The Señora came and stood at the edge of the terrace. The way her toes did not quite touch the cement was a recrimination. Her suit and hair were unenjoyably grey. One felt that she spent her life keeping away from things that would make her less neat.

Her eyes were also grey and full of self-righteousness. The neighbours would never get one on her.

'She's going to Barcelona,' said Norman. 'She suggests that instead of getting a new cleaning woman we keep hers, who lives locally. She comes in for two hours a day.'

There was a melodramatic verbal assault on Norman, and he lit his pipe and looked bland.

'What's all that about?' snapped Charmian.

'The shower. You mustn't touch the middle tap. She asks if you're going to look at the house.'

'Oh, get rid of her, Norman. Get her out! I can't think till she's out.'

Norman said goodbye and Charmian watched the woman's departing bulk with hate.

'Come in and have a look,' said Norman, but they still sat by the terrace until the after-effects of the Señora's personality had drifted out of the house. Clouds came over the top of the mountains and swallowed up the house, the children and them. Charmian flapped her arms and laughed. Norman stood up and said they were rain clouds.

'They'll get it down there,' he said, pointing to the beach.

Further away on another hill stood an old castle. At night it was lit by orange spotlights, and when the hill disappeared into the night the castle took off into the black sky and became a planet, huge and full of orange fire, gashed with craters. It dominated the village.

'Looks fake,' said Norman, condemning its everyday, grey-stone existence.

The inside of the house was cool and white-walled. Here and there were flourishes of the Señora's taste: ducks flew across a wall, paper flowers leaned dusty and deathless. Silently they removed the ducks, the calendar, the 'God Guard Our House' in gilt.

'Which room do you want, Jenny?' asked Norman.

'What about you?' she asked Charmian.

'I don't care. You choose.'

Jenny knew Norman wanted the best room but felt awful about taking it, so she spared him the guilt by taking it herself.

From the terrace they watched the ring of hills, the three roads, the gap where you could see the coast. The place belonged to its weather.

Pointing to a long, many-windowed building opposite, Norman said, 'That's a madhouse.'

It stood alone on the hill and looked deserted. The high iron gate was still closed shut.

'Whoever was in there wasn't meant to get out,' he said. 'See how high the windows are from the ground.'

'Well, it's a warning,' said Charmian. 'It will remind us to be healthy. Lots of exercise and sun and rest. You must make a decision, Jenny. You can't possibly have James and Luis here. We don't want an acrimonious scene.'

Clouds rushed over them again.

'It'll be great for the kids,' Jenny thought she heard Norman say. 'The sun and sea. We might even get something out of it as well.'

IV

The dog waited in the courtyard of the Town Hall, while Luis found out that his job application was still undecided.

He wanted the position of artistic director of the town. It was a position unknown in Gerona and the mayor was puzzled. The position had been created by Luis and would involve a lot of money, a lot of free time and a little pleasant work occasionally. The mayor reckoned it might be possible to put Luis on salary while he was actually working. In the weeks when there was nothing to do, no money.

Luis told him to forget it. Furious, he left the room.

In the corridor he met a friend of his mother.

'What are you doing here?' she asked.

'I'm applying for a licence to open a library bar in the garden of my *barraca*.'

She clapped her hands and drew her mouth in as though he was sucking a sweet. 'How wonderful. You have such wonderful ideas.'

'People can come and sit under the trees peacefully, read books and drink coffee.' On second thoughts that wasn't such a bad idea.

'You have such a lot of lovely land there. Doesn't it go down to the river?'

'Further. To the road.' The land in fact was his uncle's, but that would be resolved – when the uncle died.

'Go and see my daughter, Conchita. She's a very sweet, good girl. Very kind. She'll help you. She's the secretary of the Civil Engineer now. A very important job. You must remember my lovely Conchita. Come and take coffee with us one morning.'

It sounded too much like the fiancée set-up for comfort.

He went to the Arcada bar in the Ramblas to have a coffee with a group of artists. Mothers were always arranging to bring daughters to see him. These days they had one thing in common. They were unsought-after.

In five years art had flourished. There were over twenty galleries. Ten years ago there had been two. There were more art galleries than bars.

'I'm about to reorganise this town,' he told the group. 'I can't say much at this stage, but I should be in control of the cultural activities by the end of the week. I'm going to start an exchange of ideas with the Basque country, with the south, with Galicia. We'll have return exhibitions of art. Art treasures valued at thousands will be on show in every province. Madrid can keep its filthy face out of it.'

The big-shot talk gave little opportunity for any of the others to speak. He didn't pay for his coffee, they noticed. He never paid.

When he had no money he always went to his sister's house for lunch. On the way he bought a sheaf of tickets for the fat lottery. It was a bright, high day, full of excitement. Then Montserrat with her legs, unbending and white from the operation, came down into his mind and ruined it. Her calves, speckled with tiny pale-blue veins, looked like willow-pattern china.

His sister lived in a large apartment in the old part. Her five young children were always dressed beautifully. Today they sat on chairs along the wall and stared at him with solemn eyes, some of them squinting. His sister had married at 17. She used to be beautiful. She gave the children saucers of cream, piled with white sugar.

'Eat up, niños, then you'll get fat.'

She pinched their cheeks.

He thought suddenly of Jenny's children, their raggedness and noise. They didn't squint.

'Are you going to speak to Montserrat?' she asked. 'Speak to' meant 'propose'.

He sighed and wished she'd get the paella on the table.

'You should have children before it's too late. Our brother's got seven.'

'Yes, and look at him. He gets up before five to drive a truck for twenty hours. That's not for me.'

'You always want the good life.'

'I'll get it.'

'You haven't been exactly successful so far.'

'Don't go on,' he said irritated. 'This room is hideous. It offends me to sit in it. There's too much clutter.'

The little girls in their bleached frocks giggled, as he wheeled a padded armchair out into the passageway.

38

He put the ornate mirror by the front door and took down a gilt flower-arrangement from the wall.

The youngest child got off his chair and picked up a piece of bread that had been hardening behind it.

The mother smacked his hand. 'Caca! Caca!' she screamed. Everything children wanted to pick up was shit.

Luis was meddling with the flower pots.

'My husband arranged this room!'

'He would. The only good thing is the curtains and you've hidden them. Get rid of that sofa.'

'Get married, Luis. You know what everyone calls you? Old maid. *Solterón*. That's what they say.'

'When I win the fat one, I won't have to listen to this shit. And don't use so much peroxide on Dolores' hair. Every time I come here it's fairer. Everyone knows the child's not a blonde.'

'Camomile, I use. It brings out the colour. The hair is natural. Ask our mother.'

'That makes her the first fair child in the family for two hundred years.'

'Miracles do happen. '

Little Peter was screeching. It was light, something to be grateful for.

Norman, dark circles under his eyes, was pacing the dining-room looking for the doe doe. Adam got down from his bed and insisted on his breakfast. The other kids woke up and demanded to go to the sea. They wanted toys bought for them, chocolates, ice cream.

'What time is it?' Jenny asked.

'I don't know,' said Norman. 'Does it matter? They're up. The day's begun.'

Cornflakes on the table, eggs in the pan, milk in the doe doe, coffee in the pot. Sweet smell of the air.

'By the sun its about 6.15,' said Norman, his voice incredibly reasonable. He was wearing his new shrieking white holiday gear. Charmian lay like a dog across her bed, sleeping soundly.

'How did you sleep?'

'Didn't get much sleep, Jenny. Played musical beds most of the night with Little Peter and Sophie.'

Charmian appeared as Jenny was cutting the bread. Her eye-makeup, smudged under each eye, made her look like a panda. She was smoking already and her mood was horrible.

'Now what's happening?' She took the knife out of Jenny's hand, as though Jenny was an inefficient au pair.

'I'm giving the kids something to – '

'You've cut the bread too thick. They can't eat it like that. All right, I'll take over.'

Jenny's nerves lurched.

'Norman, I think it would be a good idea to get some Alka Seltzer,' Charmian said.

No answer.

'Norman! I said Norman!'

Silence.

Where's Norman the servant? Not sneaking out there among the trees and sunrise actually enjoying himself?

Back to the au pair. 'Where's the milk?'

'Try the fridge.'

Charmian poured some coffee, her nerves jagged. 'Where's my cigarettes? Shut up, Adam! Eat up or get out!'

Breakfast was a ghastly business. Jenny went out and joined Buttons in the servants' quarters.

'How much money have you got, Jenny?' asked Norman.

By some coincidence she had the same as he had. She knew that if she mentioned the travellers' cheques hiding in the lining of her bag she'd be lending Charmian money by the second week and, knowing the state of Charmian's overdraft, would never get it back.

Norman was disappointed. He seemed to feel that she should have more. 'Seventy-five, Jenny? We're going to have to economise.'

'Oh shut up!' said Charmian. 'This is a holiday.'

'At the rate we're going we'll only last two weeks. We'll have a kitty. Do you agree, Jenny?'

He was watching her. He suspected she had more than she'd admitted, but he was keeping pretty quiet about the extra *she* knew *he* must have. He was probably frightened Charmian would do a whirl in the hairdressers and wine-shop and he'd be keeping her after the first week.

'You give me your money, Charmian,' he was saying. 'We'll keep ours together. We'll put two-thirds in the kitty and Jenny will put a third.'

Norman was getting it all controlled. He didn't seem to want to keep her – probably hoped Jenny had enough

41

to do it. He started the game of Bluff with small meals, no eating out, no coffees out, no cosmetics, no hairdressers, cheap cigarettes, draught wine, draught brandy and no toys.

Who'll break out first with the travellers' cheques?

Montserrat's shop, as was the Spanish custom, opened at four. But she was there at three-thirty arranging the new pots from Andalusia.

'No, no, no!' shouted Luis from the alley. 'Have I taught you nothing? Putting them all together weakens their effect.'

Montserrat shivered a little. She loved it when he was hard and domineering.

'Put the little ones on the counter.'

She'd outlined her eyes the way he'd told her. Sometimes she looked almost pretty. He stood close to her and her haggard lines vanished – her flesh plumped up and pinkened. She opened up like an amorous shellfish.

Behind the velvet curtain he kissed her cheek. She tried to grab him but he dodged over to the till and opened it.

'What are you doing?' She frowned.

'Counting the money. I want to take my half for the week now. I have to go back and see the mayor and I need a new shirt. My mother – '

'Quite impossible!' She slammed the till.

'You seem to have forgotten our arrangement, *querida*. Fifty-fifty of the profits.'

Montserrat sighed. 'You're not getting one peseta,

42

Luis, unless you help in the shop. You've not put in a day's work since we opened.'

He punched the counter, and a jug fell on the floor. 'I am not a shopgirl. What do you think? If you don't want to work in here get a girl and we'll take her wage out of the profits. Get that girl of Conche's. She'll work for next to nothing and she's faithful as a dog.'

Montserrat shook her head firmly. 'You're not getting one peseta unless you work.'

'Whose idea was this shop? Who designed it? Who worked day and night supervising the builders? Our arrangement was I took half the profits once the business got going. I consider it's got going.' He looked at her sulky face and hated her.

'This is not what I understood, Luis. I thought we were partners, and as such we stay together and share the work.'

'I should have made the partnership legal. I should have gone to my lawyer. My mother told me to. She was right. She is always right about such things. So I've done all this – ' he waved at the pots – 'for nothing.'

'I kept you while you were getting the ideas developed. I paid for you to gad about all over Spain and France, supposedly looking at local pots. Business trips, you said. My father prefers to call them holidays.'

'Fine gratitude. Look what I have done for you. No man would have looked at you when I started with you. You were the outsize old maid with the bad heart who did water colours. I have taught you how to dress, how to please a man. I made you slim. I made you have your nose changed. I've given you a life sexual. I made you

43

have your elephantine legs trimmed down. I supported you through that operation.'

'Not financially, you didn't.'

'Money, money. That isn't everything. I sat with you in the hospital. I visited every day. Whose idea was it you grew your hair long?'

'If you're not working here in the shop, what are you going to be doing? '

'Ah! So that's it. Possessive,' he sneered. 'Out to crush my freedom.'

'I'm not paying you to have a good time with some other girl. What do you think?'

'There's no other girl.'

'That skinny English girl.'

'That's all over. She's back with her husband in London.' He didn't look as though he was being dishonest – but then he never did.

'Most couples who have been speaking for five years get married.'

'Now now, Montserrat. You're getting in a state.' He patted her back. 'It's not doing your heart any good. You sit down over here in the shade.' He put his arm round her. 'Our shop's looking good, no? Those pots I brought back from the south will be a big success – you see. I did the long tiring trip for us, so don't say I do nothing.' He'd certainly come back tired.

Her voice was cold as she said, 'You're not waltzing in here every week taking half the till. Sorry.'

He crossed the alley to Antonio's shop, his face glowering. 'Lend me three hundred till the end of the month.'

44

Antonio gave him 130. 'That's all I can manage. Business hasn't been quite the same since you chose to open an identical shop to mine just across the alley.'

'Don't be bitter, Antonio. There's enough trade for two shops.' He waved at the canvases, the art books, the Reeves oil paint selection. 'There's over 5,000 painters in this town.'

'Are you making much money?'

'Who knows, with her draped over the till like a bat.'

Antonio was the perpetrator of savage rumours. He didn't like it if the town was at peace. He had the yellow, disquieting eyes of a wolf, camouflaged day and night by tinted glasses. His manner was excessively gentle – he encouraged confidences. No one ever saw him eat or drink or sleep. He seemed to survive on cigarette smoke and gossip.

'Someone saw you at the Town Hall this morning. What are you trying for now? Mayor?'

'They could do worse. The swine they've got now is so short-sighted. Tries to pay me only when I'm actually hanging up the lights for the fiesta. No thought is given to the months of preparation and the ideas. Oh no. They want to treat me like a temporary typist. He can stuff the job up his pile-ridden arse! Let Madrid destroy the old town! Let them do their modernisation. I don't care.' He smacked the counter. 'I've worked for nothing all my life. Why shouldn't I have a proper salary like anyone else ?'

'So it's not going well with Montserrat?'

'I have turned her into something pleasing. I have

45

given her the energy to paint. What thanks do I get?'

'Well, here's something to cheer you up. Jenny's in town.'

Luis clapped a hand to his head. 'That's all I need. What a time to choose.'

He flopped on to a leather pouffe imported from Morocco. Its price tag fell sideways and he saw 4,000 pesetas. In spite of his distress he'd try and remember to tell Montserrat to lower their pouffe price to 3,700.

'Are the children with her?' he whispered.

'Sure. She was asking for you.'

'Has she been over there?' indicating Montserrat.

'She came from over there.'

'*Hostia!*' His life was suddenly full of dread.

He zigzagged back to Montserrat. She didn't look pleased to see him. He turned the 'open' sign to 'shut', took her behind the velvet curtain and lifted up her skirt. Afterwards she'd mellowed enough to buy him a shirt.

'Everything would be better if we were married,' she said. 'It would stop all this dishonesty and suspicion.'

'We will, I promise.'

'When?'

'When the time is right.'

They had a system. When they had decided to come away they had in mind lying in the sun on deserted beaches, walks in the hills, nightclubs, some sort of cheap mother-figure to keep the kids in line, lots of sex, wine and sleep. They had imagined that a gradual tranquil change would happen inside them.

The system was – Little Peter's early morning reveille which got the kids on their feet and whining for food. Norman and Jenny staggered among pans of boiling eggs, saucepans of coffee, bottles of juice. A cup of coffee would be taken to Charmian – 'Here's your coffee, love' – in an effort to get her up. Norman and Jenny would decide what to eat and he'd take the pushchair and empty bottles and go to the market and get the food for the day. Charmian was too pissed, or too hungover, to leave the house on foot, at least for the first days.

The cleaning woman would plod up the hill with her two children and wash the dishes with Vim, the floor with Vim, maybe even the clothes with Vim. The inside of her mouth was like the roof of a cave – long moist gums dripping with sharp irregular teeth, like icicles. She put back the ducks on the wall and the painting above the fireplace. The Señora wouldn't like it if they were moved.

Charmian got up, had two Alka-Seltzers and said she must stop drinking. She hasn't slept all night, her liver was kicking, her life was in a mess, etc. Norman came back from the market with the loaded pushchair, and the children screamed at the gate for lollies, biscuits, sweets and toys. There was no bus to any of the beaches and the nearest one was at least two kilometres down a winding road, so they took a taxi.

There was no lying down and relaxing, not with the kids going too far out to sea, trying to get across the busy road to the lolly shop, clambering up perilous rocks. It was one long nervous No. They had the I-

47

want-a-lolly, I-want-an-ice-cream, give-me-a-doughnut routine, till the taxi at 1.00 took them from the hell on the beach to the frugal repast and display of disobedience at the house.

Señora Vim stretched the official two working hours into five, and she told the time from the sky – and differently from Norman. He broke up matches to show her the Anglo-Saxon division of an hour. She couldn't see it and put her blunt face back into the sky. He paid her what she'd asked in the first place and said, 'We must get a clock.'

Charmian and Norman ate lunch quickly, hoping for a siesta. It wasn't possible because Oedipus, otherwise known as Little Peter, wasn't having any of that.

Charmian and Jenny played cards in the afternoon, and Norman went off on his own. How long would he stand it, Jenny wondered? They discussed their lives and put on make-up, and in the evening went to the village with the three eldest children for drinks and the post.

Dinner. The castle alight. 'Looks like a crème caramel,' said Charmian.

The kids were fed first and put to bed; the others started eating – tranquil, adult.

The kids got up. Norman lost his temper. Charmian put the record player on and had a bit of a dance. It wasn't what they thought it would be, but you take yourself wherever you go.

V

They watched Norman swimming out to sea, and the further he got, the faster he swam.

'I get the feeling he might go too far, like to the opposite coast and not come back,' said Jenny.

Charmian laughed. She was wearing a black, one-piece bathing suit and looked all right in it.

'Am I too fat? Tell me honestly. Is my hair all right? The colour, I mean. The style. Is my make-up O.K.? Lend me your mirror.'

Tom and Adam had learned to swim and were having a marvellous time in the water. Jenny shaded her 6.15 a.m. eyes and watched their joy.

Francis was building a sandcastle. Little Peter was causing a crisis with the family group next to them by throwing sand at their children. Charmian, it seemed, was pretending not to know him. The beach was a long splurge of noise and colour, fat lobster bodies, scorched bald heads, huge straw sunhats, empty bottles, radios playing. The sand was dirty already.

Charmian was having her morning moan. 'I don't think I can take much more of this scene. We'll have to try other beaches.'

'Would you please take your child away from my children. 'A parent's reaction to Little Peter.

The sun grew harder, hotter, and Jenny eyed the café at the top of the beach and longed for its cool, its alcohol.

'God, Jenny, I'm in a mess,' said Charmian. 'I do love Norman, but he's behaving oddly.'

'Maybe the climate doesn't suit him,' suggested Jenny.

'I'm going to write to Laurence and ask for a divorce. It can't go on. I can't sleep with Laurence any more. He'll give me a generous settlement. I want to be with Norman.'

'What does Norman say about Laurence?'

'We don't discuss him.'

'Doesn't he mind you making love with Laurence?'

'I don't know. He never asks me what goes on. I think he cuts the weekends out of his mind. In bed with Norman it's marvellous. It's the first time it's been like that with anyone.' She lay down and didn't see Little Peter swipe someone's bucket. 'I had to get away from that weekend horror. I can't tell you what it was like with the kids screaming around me all the time and Laurence violent. He beat me, yes, beat me in front of the children. No wonder they're a mess. They've seen things, awful things. I need six weeks of peace with Norman.'

Norman came out of the sea and the kids screamed around him. 'Lollies, Norman!'

'You've had lollies.'

'No, we mean ice lollies. We haven't had those.'

Norman dried his hair and looked down at Charmian. It was obvious he wanted her in spite of the sleepless nights, early mornings, hangovers, orders and Little Peter.

'The sea's marvellous. Why don't you go in?' he said.

'I don't like getting out of my depth.'

'Tomorrow we should spend all day on the beach.'

Looking at the children, already peeling and blistering, Jenny replied, 'What are you trying to do? Kill us?'

Norman made an effort to cast Jenny in the Cinderella role. 'You sit in while Charmian and I go out – '

'That's not very nice,' said Charmian. 'Here all alone.'

'Then we'll sit in while you go out.'

'And what will she do in the village on her own?' snapped Charmian. 'No, we all go out together or not at all.'

'And what about the children?' he asked.

'We'll get Señora Vim to baby-sit.'

'We haven't much money,' he reminded her. He looked at Jenny and asked, almost desperately, when James was coming. 'His being here will make all the difference.'

Jenny doubted it, due to the fact James wouldn't be there. A sample of the mealtime manners would have him booked in at the nearest hotel.

Norman, with his talent for not spending, would have fed them all on six sprats and a bowl of lettuce.

'What's this?' asked Charmian. 'The miracle of the fishes? Forget it! I want to eat.' She opened the fridge and hurled a tin of opened sardines into the rubbish.

'What did you do that for?' asked Norman, amazed. 'The tin's been opened at least two days.'

'They're all right,' he said, getting them out of the bin and putting them back in the fridge. 'Perfectly all right. I'll have them for my lunch tomorrow.'

She shuddered and put some ham on the table.

'You can't have sprats and ham. One must be for dinner,' he complained.

'We'll have something else for dinner. Some meat.'

He was aghast. 'At the exorbitant price it is here?'

2 p.m. Señora Vim still in the wash-house.

'What's she doing?' Norman wanted to know. 'Scrubbing herself down with Vim?'

'Her gums are awful,' said Charmian. 'They're all swollen. They must hurt.'

'With the money she's getting out of us she'll be able to afford the best dentist in Spain,' said Norman.

Charmian laughed. Her hair was growing thick and wavy like the sides of a corrugated shed. As it had always been straight before, with an attempted wave now and then, Jenny was baffled. No, she hadn't gone all those times to the hairdresser to get it waved but to get it straightened.

Señora Vim came through the bead curtains, panting to show how hard she worked. She waved a hand. 'Much heat.' She was trying to make them feel guilty about their leisure, and succeeded. Norman paid her for six hours and didn't complain.

The floor around the table was now much as it had been before she'd started. Lumps of hated fish hid under the chairs. There were cigarette butts and ash, spat-out lettuce, spilled juice. Sophie's chair was wet. Not competing in Little Peter's province? Señora Vim was dismayed. Should she clean it up before she went? No, no. They'd do it, Norman assured her. '*Buenas dias, Señora*. Until tomorrow.'

Norman was looking at Charmian, and Jenny suddenly saw what it was all about – she saw the warmth and the excitement.

He swallowed his lunch quickly (not that half a fish and a lettuce leaf take much time to eat) and said, 'We're going for a siesta, Jenny. Won't be long.'

Jenny sat outside in the fierce sun and looked at the hairy shrubs vibrating with light. The air quivered. The hills in the distance were smoking with mists.

Sophie was kicking Charmian's door and yelling. Little Peter asked, 'Where's my mummy?'

'Having a little rest. She's tired.'

'With Norman?'

Little Peter streaked into the house and his worst fears were confirmed. The door was locked. There were now two sets of protest outside the door, and eventually Norman came out, his cheeks glowing. He looked as though he'd had a good time.

'Sorry about that, Jenny.'

Jenny thought Norman and Charmian were beginning to look alike. Their mouths were held in the same way. The successful part of their scene happened in bed, but in San Pedro Pescador, alas, the action would have to take a different form.

On Saturday Luis was coming to see them. Jenny's

53

husband, although Luis took her away from him, had ended up finding him fascinating. He'd said, 'He's a survivor. He looks good at forty, and at sixty he'll be the same. He's clever. He assesses a scene and joins in where he'll succeed most. If he sees the scene isn't going to work, he slips out of it immediately. He's no good for you, Jenny. He'd be no good in a crisis.'

Why her husband always associated her with disaster she couldn't think.

'D'you think I'll love Luis again?' she asked Charmian.

'I don't think you've ever stopped. We're having Luis for dinner tomorrow night,' she told the kids.

'Meat at last!' shouted Adam. 'Will he fit in the oven?'

They sat peeling potatoes and drinking wine. It was dark, but the castle hadn't taken off yet – they could still see the hill. Charmian, reaching for a cigarette, found the packet empty and flung it to the ground. Norman was saying, 'Why don't you come with me to the market tomorrow, Jenny? If Charmian will get up she can look after the children.'

'Cigarettes, Norman! Where are my cigarettes?'

'Where are they?' he replied.

'I don't know,' she snapped. 'Are they in the house?'

He went in to look. 'I can't see them, sweetie.'

'Well, I must have one. Where's Little Peter, Norman?'

'By the gate.'

'He's not by the gate. Where's my baby? Norman, where's my baby, for godsake!' she shouted.

Norman's voice, calm, reassuring, came from the back of the house. 'He's all right. He's round here.'

'What's he doing?'

A pause, while Norman went to look.

A smack. A yowl. 'Naughty Peter. You're not to touch that tap.'

Little Peter came hurtling round the corner for sympathy and revenge. He pushed his head into her lap and shook with rage.

'Naughty Norman. Naughty Norman, hit baby,' she said, rubbing his hair.

'He's got to learn. Here are your cigarettes.'

'You mustn't hit him, Norman. Where's the matches? Norman, get me a match.'

Even now he avoided a row and soothed her away from a crisis by lighting her cigarette. Under his smooth face there was a lot of pain, under the non-committal statements a lot of anger. Jenny thought, he's had an unsuccessful life and now he's trying to avoid hurt and violence.

Charmian opened her bag and fumbled among her change.

'What are you doing?' Jenny asked. 'Giving him a tip?'

'You shut your mouth.' She giggled and gave him some money. 'I must have more cigarettes – and get me some Tampax and a hair conditioner. Get one for dry hair.'

'They might get the wrong idea there, what with him pushing a pram and everything,' said Jenny.

Norman laughed, a short laugh, and by the sound of it he wasn't feeling particularly amused.

55

'They're always asking why my wife isn't getting the shopping. I've told them you're busy looking after five children. They said women here with five children or more still get the shopping. They're up at seven scrubbing floors.'

She snorted. 'Well, that's tough, sweetie, because you're here with Charmian and she's not getting up at seven scrubbing floors for anyone.'

Charmian watched him rattling the pram up the hill. 'He's very good to me,' she said. 'I don't know what I'd do without him.' When Jenny didn't answer, she said, 'I don't take advantage of him. Well, O.K., sometimes. But I was born to have a hundred servants.'

When they first arrived in San Pedro Pescador Charmian, in an effort to get Little Peter and a lavatory together, said, 'This is a good chance to get him toilet-trained. I'm going to leave off his nappies.' When Jenny winced, she added, 'He's outside most of the day. Anyway, he'll learn from the others.'

But Little Peter had no intention of changing his habits. He never let having a crap disturb what he was doing. Garden, house, bed, path, were all dotted with bleached patches where they'd swilled disinfectant. Every fly in the village was now in the house. The flies had never had it so good.

Whatever nature had had in mind for Charmian, it wasn't motherhood. She should have done something using her intelligence, something academic, for she seemed to be under constant pressure to expand her life but she could never decide what to do. After university, during a bleak moment, she'd met Laurence and married him. Having Adam had been her first mistake. She'd felt that by repeating it she'd somehow change it into a success and so Sophie and Peter followed. Now she was completely trapped in domesticity and saw, only too clearly, that Laurence was not going to be trapped with her. He spent as little time at home as possible.

Francis came in triumphantly, pointing at the terrace. 'Little Peter done poo.'

There was a trail of fly-coated mess leading to the fence and, around the corner, the night-time napkin rejected and clean.

'I think I'm going mad,' said Charmian.

As Jenny walked around the back of the house, she realised that coming here was no escape. The problems were more on top of them than in London. She heard Norman murmuring something to this effect in the bedroom. Insects were buzzing and chirping, and she looked out upon mile after mile of slopes and trees and huge stars. Without thought, she stood looking into the night, and gradually the sound of the trees and insects passed into her . . . just give in . . . it seemed the best way.

Luis took the Sarfa coach to San Pedro Pescador. At all costs Jenny must be kept out of Gerona. His whole future depended on that. He hadn't sweated away two years on that shop to lose it now. But he wanted to see Jenny. He loved going to bed with her. He loved her body. How bendable it was. She excited him because she loved doing it. She was greedy. She didn't bother trying to please him. She was a taker, taking greedily what gave her pleasure.

By the time they got to the village the bus was an airless blazing tin. Passengers sat in the aisle seats, cringing from the heat. Two fainted. He had to sit at the café by the church for half an hour before he could drag himself up to the house. At least he'd be able to rest there, to eat well, and sleep. He desperately needed peace.

Norman was sitting on the terrace smoking his pipe. The house was in the sort of shape that would have Luis on the next coach out of San Pedro, and Charmian and Jenny were trying to clean it up. The day was so heavy, just keeping alive was an effort. There was no water either, except from the tap at the back of the house. Sheets hung between the trees.

'I think this is Luis,' said Norman.

Luis opened the gate. He was wearing a blue striped shirt and brown cord trousers. He was short and well-built, a physical person who loved action, loved doing things. He ran up the steps and Jenny could see that the same old magic was there. He had an attractive face with a large shapely mouth and dark eyes that slanted slightly at the corners and glowed. He was always smiling, talking. People were amazed he'd done so little, had had so little success.

Norman, in comparison, clung to his chair like a pale, powdery insect.

Norman and Luis shook hands.

'Coming from the village, this house looked deserted,' said Luis.

'Really?' said Norman, cool, guarded.

'It gave me a feeling that was odd.'

'Yes, it frequently does that to me.'

'But it looks like the house of the Little Prince up here among the clouds.'

Norman didn't answer.

Luis went on talking, but underneath he was weighing it all up. 'How do you like San Pedro, Norman?'

'I don't get a very positive reaction, Luis.'

'You are a painter. Are you doing any work here?'

'Not really.'

Norman dropped each opening. Luis pushed harder.

'Outside the village is a marvellous house. It belonged to Carmen Amaya, the great gypsy dancer. You would like it. You would find something there. I know you would.'

Another silence. Where's Charmian? Not putting on a sensational make-up? Not in there back-combing for all she's worth?

'Can I see your pictures?' asked Luis.

'There's nothing really to see,' said Norman. 'I haven't had time.'

'I know a bit about art. Montserrat Garcia Ortega is my – ' He floundered, not finding the word to describe that relationship. 'I have guided her artistic career. As you know, her work is quite established now.' He sounded proud. 'I have given her close attention.'

Jenny winced.

'I have stopped her using those sludgy greens. They were negative.'

'I'm afraid I've never heard of her.' Norman tried to sound apologetic.

Charmian swayed on to the terrace wearing a blue silk dress. She didn't have a curve in her body that that dress didn't make the most of. Her hair was the last word in grooming; her eyes sparkled.

Norman looked at her and almost fell out of his chair with surprise.

Luis and Charmian were thrilled to see each other. The kids came out from their beds and Luis gave them all a hug and a huge bag of sweets to share. Quite apart from the sweets, they loved Luis. He got on with children and handled them well. 'Come to think of it,' thought Jenny, 'he handles most things well.'

The castle lit up and Luis laughed at it. 'It's not a castle. It's a crème caramel,' he said.

'Exactly!' breathed Charmian. 'I said that. How strange we should both feel that.' Charmian was not a girl to let a coincidence go by.

Norman was at the brandy.

A bit early for him. Jenny watched him. Not having a moody is he?

Charmian, giggling, asked Luis if he wanted a drink. As her glass was empty, he filled it for her. Norman was not being the man of the house. He was opting out, at the brandy again. The dominating position was free and Luis filled it effortlessly.

'You must take a coach along the coast. You must go to different beaches every day. You must protect the children from too much sun.'

'What shall we do about dinner?' Charmian asked.

'There's vegetable soup,' said Norman.

'That's not enough,' she said.

The discussion shot into French. 'I can make some pancakes,' said Norman.

'No no.'

'Well, it's good enough for me,' said Norman.

'He speaks French,' Jenny said. 'Shall we go and eat in the village?'

'Too expensive,' said Norman. 'Look, Jenny, you and Luis go and eat in the village and we'll have the soup, Charmian.'

'Let's buy a chicken,' said Charmian.

'The dinner I've prepared is quite enough for me.' Norman was icing over.

Luis got a suggestion of the atmosphere, the correct one, and flung himself into the kitchen. 'I will make the dinner.'

'Why should you?' said Jenny. 'Let's go and eat in the village.'

'No. We'll eat together. I'll make a paella.' He wanted to be doing things. He didn't want to be passive in that atmosphere.

'What's the matter with the tap?' he asked.

'Water's cut off.'

'*Merde!*'

'Its been off two days. There's a tap at the back. Jenny showed him. 'We have to fill buckets.'

'You must get the water back on. With five children you must have water. You must go to the agency immediately.'

'Norman's been twice,' said Charmian. 'The man said he'd come and have a look.'

'You must insist,' said Luis.

'Norman's not very good at that,' said Charmian.

Before Luis even started cooking he scrubbed the stove, the draining board, the sink. 'You must wash up after every meal. That's why there are so many flies.'

Jenny didn't disillusion him, but checked the lavatory and found a used nappy lurking behind the bowl.

Hard work certainly wasn't the welcome she'd had in mind for Luis. He seemed tired and kept clearing his throat nervously.

'What time did you start work today?' she asked him.

'I was in the shop at seven. It's the market today and there were lots of tourists. The heat, the oppressive heat in Gerona, is unbearable. I work like a slave. For what?'

Charmian watched him cooking.

'He's marvellous, Jenny, he really is. He's what we need.'

She found some candles and turned off the main light. She hadn't been active at that time of night since they'd arrived.

'Tell them to sit,' said Luis. 'It must be served immediately it's cooked or it's ruined. Get the plates. It's not all that fantastic, as you haven't much food. Come and get the bread.'

'D'you think Charmian's changed?' Jenny whispered. He hadn't seen her for two years.

'It's incredible she drinks so much, because she is a woman not ugly at all.'

Norman entered, his face flushed and aggressively neutral, as Luis brought the paella in on one hand and deftly swooped it on to the table. At that point the Spanish clapped and shouted 'Olé'. This English table didn't quite manage that. Norman would only have a miniscule portion. No, he liked it very much, but he wasn't hungry – suddenly. To make up for him, Charmian ate too much. Luis was too tired to eat at all. He told them about his shop, what he sold, what his plans were, where he got his stuff. They were all impressed. Then Jenny remembered. Of course, it was Montserrat's shop, as she had the money.

'But you're not always in Gerona?' said Charmian. 'What do you do when you're not there?'

'I am designing the interior of a house outside of Barcelona,' he said glibly. 'I am the chief decorator and have to be there every day, but there are many problems. The house is already behind schedule, so alas I cannot come here as often as I hoped.'

'Who's house is it?' asked Jenny sharply.

'It is for a couple. They are getting married on the 23rd, so it must be ready then.'

Charmian ran her hands over his arm. 'You've got strong arms. They're workman's arms, but they're not bulky. Just touching you gives me energy.'

He moved his arm away and said lightly, 'You don't need energy.'

'Oh, I do. I'm without the red corpuscles.'

He laughed. 'You have force, I'm sure.'

'No. I'm a very fearful person.'

Norman stared at the black windows, while Charmian reminded Luis about the nights they'd shared in London.

'There was my husband and Jenny's husband. D'you remember, Luis? We had dinner at my flat and afterwards the men sat round the table drinking vodka and talking for hours, and Jenny and me were shoved off to sit on our own. Laurence loved Luis. He only met you twice, but he always talks about you. You must come to London again. He would love to see you.'

Norman got up. 'Goodnight.'

'Norman,' she said. 'You're not bored.'

'I find speaking French rather difficult.'

'But we're speaking English. You're drunk. Speak to Luis in Spanish. Norman speaks Spanish.'

'*Ah si?*' said Luis.

'I'll speak what everyone else is speaking.' He went to bed.

'How did it end, our evening in London?' she asked.

'You fell on your face as usual,' Jenny told her.

'I'll make some coffee, Luis,' she said.

'I'll do that,' said Jenny.

A pause for Charmian to get her priorities sorted out. She got them right, left Luis and went to Norman.

Jenny walked with Luis around San Pedro. She'd never really felt its atmosphere before, but with Luis one became alive.

When they got back, instead of going to bed he started washing up.

'Leave it.'

'Here in Spain we do not live like this. Try and get her to clean up.'

'We have a cleaning woman.'

'I wouldn't have thought it.' He started scrubbing the stove.

She put her arms round him. 'Let's go to bed. It's after one.'

'I cannot. Not with this disorder in the kitchen. I couldn't sleep. If you're not careful, you'll have every fly on the coast in here.'

VI

The next morning was bright and clear and Luis lay, arms outstretched, on the bed with the children, like birds, nesting all over him. Afterwards he went with Jenny to the village for breakfast. They ate bread smeared with oil and tomato and drank red wine.

'I used to come to San Pedro when I was a child,' he said. 'There were no tourists then, just fishermen. I loved San Pedro.' The old men sat in their line by the church, and next to them were the stalls selling plastic goods for the house and sun-dresses. 'Tourism has ruined everything. It's taken away the Spaniards' natural generosity and liveliness.'

'It's brought money.'

'Not to the people who do the work, because the taxes are enormous.'

Norman appeared, pushing the pram piled with the day's shopping, looking threatened and miserable.

Luis sprang up and called to him, but Norman didn't look round.

Luis ran and grabbed his arm.

'Come and have a drink.'

He wouldn't and withdrew into his routine.

'I have to get Charmian up. I have to get this food in the fridge. Oh yes. I've been to the agency and they're going to send a surveyor to see why the water's been cut off.'

He trundled off with the pram, its wheels beginning to squeal.

Luis sat down, preoccupied.

'He's not being rude,' said Jenny. 'It's just their affair isn't too good.'

'The children of Charmian are not right.'

'They need a psychiatrist perhaps?'

'No. It is simply a question of affection. She doesn't give it.'

'She doesn't get it.' Jenny realised that what Norman gave wasn't love. They played a tortuous game – their sexual desire, their insecurities like the antlers of sparring deer, locked together.

On the way back he bought some food and Spanish champagne. 'I will make lunch, a good one. That will cheer them.'

She didn't quite see it as the solution.

Charmian came out wearing a new and exciting swimsuit, and a full make-up. 'Let's all go to the beach.'

'No. Let's go separately,' said Norman.

'Why?'

'Because there won't be room in the taxi,' he said.

'What do you think, Luis?' Charmian asked. 'We could all sit on each other's laps.'

'You go this morning and Luis and I'll go this afternoon,' Jenny said.

Norman liked this idea. Luis liked it too – because, he said, he'd have a chance to make a marvellous lunch.

What time would they like it? What would they like for dessert?

At the bottom of the steps Charmian realised she'd forgotten her cigarettes. No, Norman wouldn't run up and get them, but there was Luis, all smiles, coming like lightning towards her, the packet on his outstretched hand. He was the day's contestant for the Cinderella role, and willing at that.

Luis said the air made him hungry, and he boiled some eggs. Looking in the mirror, Jenny saw he'd transformed her. He'd transformed Señora Vim. She rushed about laying a table on the terrace. She brought him the eggs. She wrenched the coffee pot away from Jenny.

'No no. The Spanish men like it this way.'

Napkins were got out of locked cupboards, and her gums were exposed constantly in one ecstatic smile.

The surveyor still hadn't arrived. Right! Luis, his face dark, eyes burning, would go to the agency himself.

Jenny's children were always happy with Luis. He gave them attention and care. Alas, it was always such a transitory affair. Francis sat on his shoulders. Tom held his hand as they marched down the hill and into the agency.

'Why hasn't the surveyor been?' asked Luis.

'We cannot find him,' said the agent.

'Why haven't you been?'

'I, Señor? No time.'

'My friends paid for a house with water. No water? Money back. Now!'

The man said he'd attend to the water immediately.

68

Luis leaned close to him. 'If you don't have it on in twenty minutes I will go to Gerona to my lawyer, and in twenty-four hours your agency will be out of business.'

He smacked his hand on to the desk, and papers flew up and flapped into the man's face, and then drifted slowly to the floor. Luis spun round and walked out.

Jenny and the kids followed.

The man was used to Norman. This new approach startled him, and he came out of the office fast and ran for his car.

They had a drink in the bar opposite and listened to the jukebox. Luis talked about coming to London. They'd live together, work together, travel together, have a child etc., etc. It sounded great. She'd heard it all before.

The agency man cast a long shadow over the table. 'Yes, señor, the water is back on. No, we did not have to dig up the road. There was no need.' Someone had turned off the forbidden middle tap of the shower, the tap that controlled the whole house.

Luis told Jenny this was embarrassing, but he didn't allow the man a victory. 'You should have come to the house the first day. Then they would have been saved three days of struggling without water. They have five children remember. That is what you should have done. It is your job. Still, *amigo*, have a drink.'

Norman had switched off the tap. They tracked the water shortage to his first and only shower, and he remembered being dissatisfied with the flow of water and hoping that the tap would give more speed and heat.

When they climbed the hill to the house, Charmian and family were getting out of the taxi. Luis clapped a hand to his head. 'My God! I've forgotten the lunch completely. I've forgotten them.'

Jenny realised that when a woman was with him she filled his mind. Absent, she didn't enter it.

Luis bypassed Norman's five pathetic vegetables laid out for the evening soup and hurled himself into preparations for a four-course banquet with champagne.

Jealous, Norman flopped on to his bed, face to the wall, and stayed there.

'What is the matter with Norman?' Luis asked.

'He's not very well. It's nothing,' said Charmian, as Luis advanced towards the bedroom. 'Nothing at all.'

'Is it your stomach, Norman?' he shouted through the door.

No answer. 'He'll be all right,' said Charmian, leading him back to the kitchen.

'It's the heat,' Luis said. To Jenny, he added, 'And the drink. You can't drink like that in this heat.'

He prepared a magical tisane with herbs from the garden, and when the women were busy with their evening make-up competition he sneaked it into Norman. Can't have one of the family cutting himself off like this.

Norman wouldn't touch it. Furious, he kept his face to the wall and wanted to be left alone. Luis insisted he wouldn't get any better till he took it. Charmian rescued a rather dangerous situation by drinking it herself. She'd got a terrible liver pain suddenly.

The meal was ready. Norman appeared in the doorway, perhaps willing to join them. Unfortunately Charmian, at that moment, was saying, 'His food is great. This is what we need, Jenny. Luis certainly gives us what we need.'

Norman lurched back to bed.

Luis was fascinated by Charmian's abandon, especially when she got going on the liquor. She talked about politics, French and Spanish; what living in France was like; what living with Laurence was like; and she concluded the rather provocative exchange by saying, 'Let's go to a discothèque. Us three. You'll let me dance with Luis, won't you, Jenny? Just for a bit.'

'What about the children?' asked Luis.

'Norman can babysit. I expect you're a very good dancer, Luis.'

'No, no.' Luis was shocked. 'We can't do this to Norman. He'll leave immediately.'

'I doubt it,' she said.

'Well, I would.'

She stood up. 'Let's go.'

'No, Charmian.'

Charmian took hold of his arm and called him bourgeois.

'Ridiculous,' said Jenny.

'I understand exactly what she's getting at,' said Luis.

'Don't we all.'

71

They went out on to the terrace, and she began another episode of helplessness.

' I don't know what to do. I know my kids are cracked up . . .' Her hands were all over him. 'You're so strong. I'm sure you could help.'

Jenny said, 'Keep off Luis. Don't touch him.'

'I didn't realise what I was doing. I'm a bit pissed up.'

'A marvellous excuse.'

'Jenny, you're becoming bourgeois.'

Luis laughed and pushed their heads together. 'Come on. Don't fight. You are sisters of the soul. You have the same vices. Jenny, on reflection, has more virtues.'

Jenny was shocked when he said he couldn't stay.

'I thought you were going to spend several days. That's what you said in the spring. That's why I took this house.'

'I regret, not this time. I have to finish the house in Barcelona.'

'Which house?'

'The one I told you about the other night. And I have to get back because my mother is ill.'

'What's wrong with her?'

'Everything is in plaster,' he said quickly. 'She had a fall. In this heat plaster is dangerous. Her heart is terrible. Last week she had a heart attack. I must be there.'

'I'll come with you. Charmian and Norman will watch my kids.'

'No, no, no! It is far too hot for you in Gerona. And I am very busy. You stay here in the cool. It is much better for your nerves.'

'My nerves are all right.'

For a moment he'd forgotten Jenny was symptomless. It was always easier when his women had disabilities. He could slip in and out and around their rest times, their early nights, their migraine headaches in darkened rooms.

'Heat like that in Gerona would kill you. You English can't take it. I'll come out soon, yes?'

He borrowed five hundred pesetas and took a taxi so as to be in time for lunch with Montserrat and her sister.

The children stood in a line and waved to him. They were sad. Adam ran and gave him a drawing. Luis waved one last time as he curved down into the village.

The morning was so oppressive they longed for a storm. Jenny's life was made up of waiting for Luis. He would come, stay briefly and then be gone again. The terrace was covered with Charmian's dog-ends and white patches where they'd swilled the bleach. Little Peter seemed to have shitted over every paving stone in the place. Insects were croaking.

Charmian came out and, seeing Jenny's ransacked face, said, 'God! You look the way I feel.'

'I'm glad someone feels good,' she said bitterly.

'Where's Luis?'

'Gone.'

'Just like that? No wonder you look awful.'

Norman came out with some coffee. 'Gone, has he?'

'There's one who's pleased,' said Charmian.

'Not at all.'

'Norman doesn't like people. Half the time he doesn't even see them. They're just shapes, part of a pattern.'

'Not you,' said Jenny.

'Perhaps I do stand out, though half the time I don't think I get through. Luis certainly does something for you, Jenny. When he's here, you're transformed. When's he coming back?'

'He said in a few days.'

'But James will be coming. What will you do?'

'I'll put him off. James, I mean.'

'I hope it'll be worth it. I hope Luis will come again.'

'It'll be worth it.' She didn't really have any choice. She never did where Luis was concerned.

Montserrat's face was white and puffed up. She'd been crying for hours. He said hello and re-arranged the pots.

She didn't answer.

'Shall we go to the lunch?' he asked. 'Montserrat!'

Her pale eyes leaked more tears.

'Has something happened? Is it your heart?'

'Where were you last night?'

He shrugged. 'I was looking for something in the country.'

'What?'

'A house.'

'Who for?'

'Us.'

She shot up and got hold of him. He'd never seen anyone's eyes so full of joy. 'Where, where is it?'

'You'll see. It's a surprise.'

So in spite of himself he became engaged to Montserrat. She was very happy. Her parents took them out to celebrate at a small *restaurant typique* in the hills. Any pleasure he might have had was crushed by one nagging fear. Jenny might arrive at any moment. It was a restaurant she knew well. He remembered tenderly the summer he'd spent with her, the evenings they'd sat there at the bare scarred table, drinking wine and planning their future.

But Jenny was having another sort of entertainment . . .

No day or night passed without the children's demands and disobedience. Every meal was a food-slinging orgy. Norman would sometimes make attempts to get on top of the situation and, taking a burst of energy from his pipe, say, all brightness and authority, 'Look, let's get the kids out of the house all day today. They mustn't get bored . . .' Now he said, 'This village is expensive: Apparently there's a market in Palafrugell on a Sunday that's very cheap. We could get everything for the week. What do you think, Jenny?'

'Meat wouldn't keep a week,' Charmian told him before Jenny could reply.

'Well, Luis is coming tomorrow, and on Sunday he, I and Jenny could go and get the bulk of the groceries.' Seeing her expression he added, 'You could come too, sweetie, if you felt up to it.'

The night was mauve and peaceful, the air silky. It was no time for a row. Charmian said, 'Norman's got the scene all wrapped up. He doesn't refer to me at all. He's taken my money. He chooses the food. I never get a look in.'

'You were a bit pissed up the first few days – remember, sweetie?' he said sharply.

'He's showing another side of himself,' she said to Jenny and opened another bottle of wine.

'I wouldn't drink any more, Charmian,' he said.

'Why not?'

'You can't take it any more.'

'I'd like a thousand pesetas, please.'

'Why?' He sounded surprised.

'Just to have the feel of my money again. I'm going to Barcelona for a day. Alone.' Rivals. Rivals. That would put Norman in his place.

'She went through Laurence's money in three years and hasn't a thing to show for it,' he told Jenny.

'Except a rotten liver. But we had a marvellous time. You can have a marvellous time with Laurence.'

A pause. Come on Norman, thought Jenny, suffer.

Little Peter screeched.

Norman sighed.

Nothing happened, except the sky got blacker and Peter went on screeching.

Charmian poured another drink.

'What are you going to do about him?' asked Norman.

'What can I do?'

'Go in to him.'

'You go.'

He puffed on his pipe furiously. Little Peter flashed out of the house and flung himself at Charmian.

'All right petty, all right,' she comforted him.

He stopped screaming, got into her lap and smiled angelically. It would be like any other night.

Jenny stood up and said she'd get the food.

'First Little Peter goes to bed,' said Norman.

Little Peter climbed on to the wall and did a dance.

'Naughty baby. Naughty baby. Making Norman cross. Naughty Norman, cross with baby.' Charmian's face was flushed, eyes bright.

'Charmian!' His voice quivered with anger.

'He won't go to bed. It's no good,' she said impatiently.

'I want some time without these children. They're up before seven. It's fourteen hours of HELL, Charmian. I've had enough.'

Peter jumped off the wall and his bottle fell from between his teeth and smashed.

'Oh Christ!' she murmured. 'That's it. What are we going to do, Norman?'

'Give him another one.'

'I haven't got another one.'

'Surely, seeing it's such an indispensable part of his life, you'd have several.'

Little Peter pointed to the glass and said forlornly, 'Doe doe.'

'I'd get it picked up, Charmian, before someone lacerates a toe,' said Jenny.

She bent slowly and nearly toppled out of her chair. Jenny picked up the pieces and Norman swept the terrace, his tan disappearing into the white of his rage. Now all they had to do was to get Little Peter separated from Charmian and eat, so Sophie chose that moment to run on to the terrace. Squeals of delight.

'I'm not standing for it,' said Norman.

'He won't go to sleep without his doe doe.'

'He'll have to. He's nearly three.'

The wine was finished, so she reached out for the brandy. The last piece of the hill dissolved into the black sky and the old castle soared.

Little Peter tugged Sophie's nightdress, and they ran round the side of the house, shouting. As James would say, if he was there, 'Why let them go on doing something they know isn't right? It isn't fair to them. Knowing where they'll be stopped gives them security.' He'd certainly say it. He'd said it often enough to Jenny. She suggested something like that to Charmian.

'I haven't the energy or the power. He's much stronger than me, Jenny. He overpowers me – Little Peter, I mean.' She giggled. Perhaps Norman would clout her one now. A smack seemed to be called for somewhere.

As Little Peter hurtled round the table for the seventh time, Norman snatched him up. 'Get Sophie, Charmian,' he said, and he rushed Little Peter off to bed. All the kids were awake.

Charmian came back on to the terrace and poured another drink.

A brief silence. Then Little Peter started yelling for his doe doe.

When she didn't move, Norman said, 'Go in to him, Charmian.'

'You go.'

'He needs you, not me. You're his mother, remember.'

'There's no point. He wants his bottle. Go to the chemist and get him one, Norman. Then he'll shut up.'

'It's closed.'

She poured another drink. There came a point of no return with Charmian, usually about the time she started on the brandy.

'I'm like an unpaid nanny,' he said bitterly.

'He doesn't have to throw himself into the domestic scene like this,' Charmian told Jenny. 'No one's asked him to.'

'Well, who would get them breakfast? You? And if I didn't get up, Jenny would have to do it all. It's not fair. I'm working all the time. I'm supposed to be having a holiday.'

Charmian started giggling and couldn't stop. In the house Little Peter was crying and couldn't stop.

'Go into him,' said Jenny.

'What can I do?'

'Smack him!' said Norman.

'Talk to him.'

'Nurse him.'

'Do whatever you feel you must do to stop him,' Jenny said.

'You both seem to have plenty to say,' said Charmian.

Norman got up and stood in front of her. He wanted to hit her. Terrified, he smothered the impulse and lit his pipe. In recompense for his rage, he said – gently, almost to himself – 'Do what you can.'

Still thinking he was going to hit her, she looked up, saw he wouldn't, couldn't, and said, 'Oh, get off my back.' She had another drink. At least the misery would soon be hidden from her by unconsciousness. 'Anyway, what's all this, Jenny? I didn't know you were so fantastically organised yourself.'

'I've had to be.'

'This doesn't sound like you, Jenny,' she said. 'You sound pompous. Like James.'

'Life like this is hell.'

'Don't I know it.' She suddenly seemed clear-headed. She lit a cigarette. 'I've tried hitting him. It doesn't do any good at all.'

'You've spoilt him,' said Norman.

'Oh, do shut up.'

'You either go to him, Charmian, or I'm leaving,' he said.

She didn't and he didn't leave either, although a case was taken down and packed. At some point Little Peter, covered in tears and sweat, without his doe doe, fell asleep in the doorway. Norman lifted him up, tenderly, and put him to bed. About the same time Charmian fell off her chair. As James had said, 'If you want a nihilistic gesture, Charmian will provide it.'

VII

Although he tried to stop it, a formal announcement appeared in the local paper. Luis' mother, on behalf of her son, asked permission from the parents of Montserrat Garcia Ortega for her son to 'talk' to her. Permission was granted, and Luis officially took coffee with the family at 11.30 each morning. Montserrat bought her own engagement ring, but he put it on her finger.

Luis' mother, in fact, had nothing to do with it. She hated all fiancées. Secretly, though, she admitted that it was his only solution. She could see that he wasn't going to make any money for himself. She was tired of newspaper in the lavatory, patching up frayed cuffs.

Luis couldn't get back to San Pedro Pescador for nearly a week, and two urgent telegrams from Jenny waited at his home. One said, 'I need you.' The second, 'Fuck you.'

When he went into the shop to claim his fifty per cent of the week's profit, he was surprised to find 'asking for her hand' had made no difference.

'Why do you need the money? I can't pay for everything.'

'I have to buy trousers to see the mayor.'

'You seem to be re-stocking your wardrobe for this – this elusive meeting. Why d'you want to see him?'

81

'To arrange to get a licence, so we can open a small bar in the back of the shop.'

'To try and get another job, you mean. I know you've been running around him for something. You're going to leave me, I know it.'

'Hostia! How much more of this do I have to take?' He rushed to the till and opened it. But she'd already thought of that. It was empty.

His mother would only give him fifty pesetas, so he had to go by bus.

For some reason the bus tried to include every village within a ten mile radius, so it didn't get to San Pedro for nearly two hours. The convoluted ride in the heat made him ill. Twice the bus had to wait while he stood at the roadside waiting to see if he was going to be sick.

In San Pedro he had to have three brandies before he could face the house. He overheard a strange thing about some English school teachers living on the coast who ran a Lesbian brothel. They kept a small masochistic male servant whom they were trying to turn into a woman. It made him laugh. He wondered who they were.

The village was strange, because it had no atmosphere. The main feature was the square, in which there was a church, its beauty marred by a new squat *bureau de change*. Along the side of the church, the old men – redundant fishermen – sat and watched the village changing. There were three lines of taxis, two cafés – neither particularly Spanish (there was a Spanish bar but they didn't want tourists in it) – a small market selling sundresses and hats. A boutique, a nightclub and a couple of house agencies all helped to take away the village's character. The streets were narrow and cobbled, and there were too many cars all driven by maniacs. On the way out from the village there were several alleys, and the atmosphere there was Spanish at last. People sat outside playing cards and drinking; a lot of singing was done; they had time to enjoy things, and they seemed a million miles away from the racket in the square. Before the village had resorted to tourism, there had been fishing and agriculture and a cork factory. Now the village was full of Spaniards come up from the south to make money, and they didn't belong there, any more than the tourists. San Pedro Pescador had an uncertain feel about it.

Luis covered several biscuits lavishly with Nestles milk.

'Ugh!' said Charmian. 'How disgusting!'

'How bad for you,' said Jenny.

'Do you English never enjoy sugary milk?'

'Not if we've any sense. You're fat as it is.'

'But I'm losing weight. If I go below 90 kilos, it is dangerous for me.'

He was always frightened of thinness. Jenny's lack of flesh terrified him.

Charmian said, 'I hear your partner Montserrat is very rich.'

'It's all comparative,' he replied.

'How did she get her money, exactly?'

'From bread. They own a string of bakeries. Our shop used to be a breadshop, till I convinced them we could double the profit in a more interesting way.'

'Do you like her?' Charmian asked.

'I've known her since we were children.'

'Is she a virgin?' Charmian asked. She reddened. Someone had kicked her under the table, hard.

'I do not know personally, but I'm sure she is. It would not be correct for a good Spanish girl to be otherwise.'

'In England it's bad enough to be old and unmarried. But old, unmarried and a virgin – that's the end.'

'To be an old maid here is quite acceptable, as long as you are intact.'

'Still, she must be quite a catch,' murmured Charmian.

'The streets stink, the drains smell,' said Norman loudly, so turning Charmian towards her next favourite subject, Spanish squalor.

'In England it would not be allowed,' said Charmian. 'No wonder Little Peter's shitting all the time. And that olive oil. The smell! The Spanish really are filthy.'

Little Peter came in, covered in brown muck. Everyone breathed easier when it turned out to be a chocolate milk.

'A Spanish child would never look like him,' said Luis.

'They will,' said Charmian. 'They're just not liberated. Anyway, it's not filth. It's natural. I know the Spanish are obsessed about throwing the bleach around, but I think they should give more thought to the beaches. They're unhealthy.' She waved a finger at him. 'Blocked drains, indescribable cooking smells and disgusting beaches. That's the Spanish.'

Luis followed Jenny into the bedroom. 'Can you ask Norman to get me another tin of Nestles milk when he goes shopping?'

She held out her hand. He took it. She meant she wanted money.

'I regret I have none.'

'None?' She was astounded.

'I have thirty pesetas for my bus back to Gerona.'

'Why the hell didn't you bring any?'

'I haven't got any.'

'What about the house you're decorating?'

'What house?'

She watched him. He bit his lip. He shuffled desperately, the lies of the past weeks.

'The house you're supposed to be doing outside of Barcelona.' Her voice was icy. 'The reason you can't spend much time here. Remember?'

'Oh that. I don't get paid till it's finished.'

'Well, the shop.'

'It is not yet making a profit, so I can't touch that.'

'You said that in the spring. Surely you got paid for building it?'

'I did not take one peseta.'

She sighed. 'You're always so self-sacrificing, except here.'

'Listen. Montserrat offered me several thousand pesetas when she knew I was taking a holiday, but I wouldn't take them. I would not touch her money.'

'Why not?'

85

'Because she's hard and ordinary. I cannot support a woman who is hard and ordinary.'

Hard and ordinary with the bank account, she thought.

'Do you have an affair with her?'

'Certainly not. I told you not. I would not lay as much as one finger on her.'

'Why not?'

'Why should I?' He shrugged. 'Making love is particular, isn't it?' He pulled her beside him on the bed. 'I couldn't enjoy myself here with you if I thought that hard woman was paying for it.'

'He always rushes back,' said Charmian. 'What's in Gerona?'

'He said his mother's ill.'

'Well, there's his sister and brother. What happens when he takes these long business trips collecting ceramics for the shop? I don't believe it. I bet it's Montserrat. I bet there's more to that than meets the eye.'

'They're probably married,' said Norman.

When he came back at the weekend Jenny asked, 'Do you sleep with Montserrat?'

'I told you I didn't.'

'I'd rather know the truth.'

'I have never touched her. Never. It is only a business affair.'

'Don't you find her attractive?'

'Well . . . she has nice eyes.'

'I wished we lived together. I wish I had your child.'

'We will. We will. When the time is right.'

86

Jenny overheard something in the Spanish locals' bar that made her head spin. The man from the house agency was saying, 'Mr Water-Shortage is 'talking' to Montserrat Garcia Ortega.'

'Never.'

'Certainly, it's true. I read it in the paper.'

'Has he been to her house yet?'

'He's entered the house, yes. He was invited for coffee to meet the parents.'

Jenny didn't wait for a coach but took a taxi to Gerona and went immediately to see Antonio.

'Is he getting married?'

Antonio chuckled. 'He hasn't time for a woman. He's too busy being the conscience of the artists of Gerona. I hear he's just formed them into a group. He's the director.'

'Let's hope he gets director's pay.' Jenny flopped on to a Moroccan pouffe and fanned her face. She was breathless and sweating.

'You shouldn't have come to Gerona. Montserrat's got a bad heart. Every time you arrive she has an attack. In the end you might kill her.'

'Does he have an affair with her?'

'He does something with her. She looks almost female when he's around.' He leaned towards her. There was nothing he liked more in the world than spreading gossip. His voice was silky. 'People say, she hasn't given herself completely. She's a proper Spanish girl and it would finish her chances of marriage if she was not a virgin. But I think she's been silly and burnt her boats.'

'Will the shop do well?'

'Yes, because of her. She's put money into it. She won't abandon her money. Oh no. She's in there first thing in the morning till late at night. She's ambitious – not the least of her ambitions being to marry him.' He stared at her windows. It was hard to see anything, crammed as they were with eye-catching knicknacks from every corner of Spain. 'She paints terrible pictures,' he said confidentially. 'Luis, of course, is very much the proprietor. On Saturdays he stands in the doorway looking important. He's above all that buying and selling. The truth is, he's workshy. Always has been. He won't work. Thinks it's beneath him.'

'Is he in Gerona?'

'He was in here, in my shop, just now. They've had a quarrel because she caught him stealing her cement. He ordered some to start making a bar behind the shop, but half of it was delivered to his *barraca*. He's obviously doing something up there she doesn't know about. She happened to pass that way and saw it piled outside his gate. Why should she pay for something that's going to free him from here? He said there must have been some mistake. She's right, of course. If he had something – anything – that made him a living, he wouldn't need her.'

For a moment Jenny wished desperately that she had money, but even that wouldn't pin him down.

'He's a funny man. He's clever, but only up to a point. He always gets caught. He was in here complaining bitterly about the state of the country. He's formed this association to protect Catalan art and wants me to

88

make a donation. I tell him I have enough here trying to survive with all the competition from his side of the alley. He'll end up mayor. That's what he wants. He's like a mole. He goes underground. No one sees him for weeks. Then he pops up with some startling new scheme. I didn't see him for nearly a year: then up he comes right opposite me, copying my shop, my ideas. If I don't watch it, he'll pop up right here in my shop. He runs round and round Montserrat, but she's no fool. She gives him one peseta here, one peseta there.'

'Will he marry her?'

'Perhaps. If he gets to fifty and his teeth are dropping out and his hair is dropping out and no one will look at him. Yes, then he might.'

His mother opened the door. Her face darkened when she saw the English girl. Jenny was taken aback to see her on her feet and not in plaster. There was no sign of any heart condition, at least not a medical one. Hatred, of course, made itself felt.

'How are you after your accident, Señora?'

'The only accident is you, English girl. Go away. My son will marry a Spanish girl, a proper girl, with big breasts and black hair.'

The description did not fit Montserrat. 'Where is he?'

'He has gone to Paris. He went on the afternoon train. He is getting a job there.'

'When will he be back?'

'He said in October.'

Meanwhile Luis was naked with Montserrat behind the velvet curtain.

'Turn over. Let me do it that way.'

She opened her eyes. 'How dare you! What are you thinking? Do you think I'm a whore?' Correct Spanish women seemed only to feel all right in the most conventional position. He suggested other alternatives.

'Certainly not!' She sounded as though a bucket of water had been flung over her.

VIII

Charmian's first visit to a bar enriched the Lesbian brothel rumour. Her appearance, slightly drunk, in the local café wearing a transparent blouse and no bra caused a reaction that could be heard the other side of the square. People thought a football match must be showing on television and the favourite side had scored a goal. When the whistles and shouts calmed down, Charmian ordered a double brandy. Jenny, properly clothed, sat in the corner, unnoticed.

The barman said, '*Ven a joder conmigo.*'

Charmian said, 'Yes, but not too much. And a little ice.'

'Oola!' screamed the men. 'She wants to cool down.'

'*Le voy a joder como un leon,*' said the barman.

Charmian thought he must be asking about her sign of the zodiac. She nodded enthusiastically. 'Yes, I am a leo. How clever you are.'

The men squealed with laughter as they edged up to Charmian. One taught her to say, '*Yo jodo como una leona.*'

Thinking it meant 'My sign is leo', she said it several times.

Jenny shuddered.

'*Ven acá, mala puta. Voy arrancarte la melena del cono*,' said the barman.

'Aren't they friendly in here?' she said to Jenny.

Luis couldn't give any satisfactory reason why his mother was out of plaster so quickly. 'It was hot, so she took it off.'

'There's usually a bit more to it than that,' said Jenny. 'You make it sound like taking off a coat.'

He turned to Charmian and changed the subject. 'Have you learned any Spanish?'

'How can she?' said Norman. 'She's hardly been out. She's flaked out on the bed with a hangover most of the time.'

Charmian leaned across and said to Luis, '*Yo jodo como una leona.*'

There was a nasty silence. Luis shifted uneasily and looked the other way. 'The castle is about to be transformed into a crème caramel,' he said quickly.

Charmian was waiting for him when he came out of the lavatory. 'What do you see in Jenny?' she asked slyly.

'I have known her a long time.'

'Do you love her?'

'In my fashion.'

'He always answers so pat, it's impossible to believe him,' she told Norman afterwards.

'Jenny's hung up. She doesn't see him as he is,' he replied.

'Try and get her to wash Little Peter's face before he goes out,' Luis said before he left. 'And make sure he wears pants. He can't be naked on a beach. The Spanish don't understand him. He'll give the house a bad name.'

'They're good at that, at gossip. I heard some about you the other day,' said Jenny.

He flinched, but his voice was joky as he asked, 'Who could do that?'

'They said you were engaged to Montserrat Garcia Ortega.'

'Absolutely untrue. People are always making rumours about me.'

'Why don't we get married?'

'When the time is right we will.'

'When's that?'

'When the shop is flourishing. Then I can go. I'll have enough money to get a girl to look after my mother,' he sighed.

'Why not now?'

He stood up and forgot the thousand-peseta note she was lending him for a taxi. The thought of the altar could get between anything. 'It's a nice idea. Yes. But it takes a long time here. You can't just walk into a church.'

Put out, she said, 'I'm not that impatient. I'll stay here.'

'It's different for us Spaniards. Whew! It's hot in here.'

After an absence of only four days Gerona looked mysterious. Luis was always finding new things in it to love. But he couldn't loiter long in the Paseo Arqueologico. The first thing he had to do was placate his mother. The second, make love to Montserrat.

He was too clumsy for the first and too exhausted for the second. Although it was Sunday, Montserrat's face hung sadly among the pots in the shop window, like a lantern gone out. He told her he'd been decorating a small house outside Barcelona.

'Where?'

'It's a surprise.' When he kissed her, she glowed. When he was with her she was almost pretty. He gave her a transfusion of attractiveness, but he was never there long enough for it to be anything other than temporary.

He told his mother the house-outside-Barcelona story, in which he was now well practised.

'You've been with that English girl,' she said, before he could finish.

'Never.'

'Oh yes you have. I can see it in your face. You're worn out.'

'Where's my dog?'

'Gone,' she said harshly. 'It's a sign. It's just the beginning. If you carry on with her it'll end in trouble. I've warned you before about such women. I've always been right. That path is a bad one. Get off it.'

IX

After Luis' visits, Charmian was discontented with the usual routine. She wanted to go out. They had Sardanas in the square on Saturday night, So Señora Vim came to baby-sit and brought her whole family for company. They sat in a ring on the terrace and Jenny met uncles, cousins, nieces.

The three of them went down to the square, which was packed. By the church a small band of wind instruments and drums was playing the haunting Sardana music. The dance, which was performed in a circle, holding hands, and had two rhythms—one for the feet, another for the arms—was dignified, yet full of enjoyment. It looked simple, but if you didn't know how to do it you could make a horrible mess, as was being demonstrated by a group of drunken tourists on the left.

Jenny was enchanted. 'Let's join in.'

'The only question is where,' said Charmian.

The best dancers were in the middle circle. They used the minimum movement but had rhythm and feeling.

Jenny started towards them.

'Where are you going?' Charmian asked. 'They're

far too good. Let's join in here,' and she indicated a less talented circle. 'But supposing we go to join in and they won't let us?'

'Yes, we'd look pretty stupid,' Jenny agreed.

There were rows of people sitting on chairs, watching.

'Let's have a drink,' said Norman.

They had a drink and were ready to start, but the music stopped and everyone took a rest.

'When it starts again, get in next to the boy in the middle circle,' Jenny said.

'You always join in where the best is happening,' said Charmian. 'I suggest we join in somewhere less good.'

'But the better the people we're with, the better we'll be. Don't you see?' said Jenny.

'I don't. The better the people are, the more clumsy we'll look.' The dance started again. 'Do you want to join in, Norman?'

'Sure. When this one's over.'

'O.K. Let's go.' Jenny moved towards the centre.

'It'll be better here,' said Charmian, pulling towards the furthest circle. 'We'll practise here. Then, when we feel confident, we'll go to the centre.'

They stood near the circle. The dancers were all Spanish and ignored them.

'Go on.'

'No, you.'

'Come on.' Norman moved towards them and Charmian remembered his dancing style.

'No, no. Another drink.' On the way to the bar she said, 'He dances like a grasshopper.'

Another brandy and Charmian's eyes were veined and she was ready for anything. She chose the group almost out of the square altogether. 'I'm feeling a bit pissed up, so I might stumble. Let's practise with these.'

'But they're so bad we'll never learn,' Jenny said, still eyeing the boy in the centre.

'Come on,' said Norman, taking their hands, and the circle opened for them.

'No, I can't,' said Charmian.

Norman sighed. 'She never will join in. It's the same at parties.'

Charmian turned to Jenny. 'He thinks I don't enjoy parties, because I won't dance with him. Have you seen him dance?'

'Come on. Let's copy these on our own,' said Jenny. They held hands and stood outside the circle.

Norman gave an optimistic leap, two yards in the air, and Jenny could see what Charmian meant.

She started giggling.

'Come on,' he said. But by now Charmian and Jenny felt so inferior their feet would hardly leave the ground.

'Let's have another drink,' Charmian murmured.

Norman's face was dark, eyes icy.

'You're never happy, Norman,' she said.

'I thought I was happy with you.'

'You haven't enjoyed yourself in San Pedro at all.'

'I'm spending most of my time trying to keep my legs from shaking and my stomach from throwing up.'

'You're incapable of enjoyment,' she said.

'You're incapable of joining in.'

'I'd join in if I had the right partner.'

'There's always an "if". It's lucky there isn't the right partner, or you might have to join in.'

'Don't worry. I would, if I was with a good dancer.'

'What's that supposed to mean?'

'I can't dance with you, Norman. I never have been able to. I wish Luis was here. I'd join in then.'

A pause. Then he made a dramatic slap at her hair. Jenny thought he was swatting a fly. He was giving her one on the ear.

'God, Norman. Stop that!' She was outraged.

'You asked for it.' He was shaking.

They had another set of drinks. 'Now come on,' Jenny said. 'Stop hesitating, stop thinking, stop weighing it up! Let's join in!'

'You join in, Jenny,' he said. 'All she can do is loll against the bar.'

But by now she was so full of inadequacies she couldn't have joined in if someone had asked her. Not that anyone was going to. They kept themselves to themselves on Saturday nights and, considering the average tourist, who could blame them?

'Come on,' she said. 'If we don't do it now we never will.'

They were great, the Spanish. Old men, big fat women, children, all dancing, skilful and beautiful. By the time she'd got the glass out of Charmian's hand, the band was packing up and going home.

'Next time I will,' she said. 'Next time we're going to join in.'

Luis' cool bedroom made thought possible. He lay

on the silk bedcover and let the white sugary walls soothe him. Seeing Jenny was dangerous. Shutting her in a remote village up the coast had seemed to be the answer. But she always had such freedom of movement. Bus travel in the murderous heat of the afternoon meant nothing to her. He supposed it was because she was English.

Then he heard his mother cough. So she was in. Why hadn't she answered when he called? She was lying on her bed, a great mound of misery. 'You've been with that English broomstick again. What d'you waste your time on her for? She's a slut dragging her children over here after you, leaving her husband. The whole of Gerona's talking. Wait till your barren *novia* finds out. Or her miser father. She'll end badly, you see.'

'Who?'

'Both of them. But especially that English tramp. You should marry a Spanish girl, a proper girl with plenty of juice and big breasts. Not that withered stick.'

'All right, I'll marry Maria,' he said provocatively.

'She's not right,' said his mother immediately. 'She's not serious. That English girl will end badly. Make sure you're not with her when it happens.'

He went out shivering.

Montserrat wasn't in the shop. He crept in and took four hundred pesetas from the till. The velvet curtain moved and she said, 'People tell me there are some indecent English women up the coast. I wondered if they meant your friend.'

'Why should they? She's untidy. Nothing else.'

99

'I suppose you've been decorating our marital home.'

'It's too hot in here.' He went and stood in the doorway.

'I've given you the best years of my life!'

'What do you mean? I've made you what you are. I've given you style. When I met you, you were an elephant. You can go anywhere now. Well, almost anywhere.'

'I'd like to marry next month.'

'Too soon. I mean, what will people think?' he added hastily. 'We've only just got engaged.'

'I don't care any more what anyone thinks,' she blazed. 'You fix the date, or I'll re-think this partnership. You won't get one peseta.'

'You'd be nothing without me. With me you've produced pictures that people buy.'

'I painted them. Not you!'

'You may paint them, but I am the brush. Everyone in Gerona says I am your brush. If I leave you, your artistic career will be finished.' He threw the four hundred pesetas on to the carpet and went to the only place where he knew he could relax. The brothel.

He'd been going to the Barrio Chino since he was nineteen. He only paid when he had the money. He lay on the girl's bed and thought of Jenny. Jenny had a great sense of herself. He admired that. He remembered the first time he'd seen her. She'd come to Gerona hitch-hiking when she was sixteen. Early one morning he'd walked up the Calle Forsa to the cathedral, and sitting on the top step by the engraved doors was a frail, fair figure. As he got nearer the sun suddenly came out, just one solitary shaft among the clouds. It beamed directly on to the figure. The sun had gone in, but now and again it still shone, even after twelve years. Now he thought of her as the Queen of Chaos. Every time she came into his life disasters happened. She was like a comet that passed now and then, causing havoc.

Montserrat was so melancholy she didn't smile, speak or even try to sell things. She spent the days behind the velvet curtain gulping heart tablets. Even talk of their forthcoming wedding didn't cheer her – not even his promise to bring the date forward from the late summer of the following year to before Christmas of this one. His future looked shaky. He could see he'd have to make some desperate gesture. The one he chose – sending her home to rest while he took over the shop – pleased her father, who gave him a box of cigars.

Luis arranged the pots differently and leaned in the doorway, glaring across at Antonio's shop. He counted Antonio's customers, tried to see what they were buying. 'Son of a whore,' he muttered. 'I sweat my guts out working here. Is this what my life has come to?'

Just as he was closing for the afternoon – 'Everyone else has a siesta. Why shouldn't I?' – a dentist's wife, elegant and middle-aged, sauntered in to look at the pots.

'Is there anything you have in mind, madam?'

She took off her dark glasses and smiled at him. 'Nothing in particular. I'm just looking.'

He was on to the style in a flash and hovered near as she fingered the trinkets. 'What nice pots you have. I

101

like things big.' She peeked behind the velvet curtain, saw the back of the shop was empty. 'Been open long?'

'I don't know, madam. I don't work here. The shop girl is ill, so I said I'd keep an eye on things.'

She picked up a tin jug. 'I'll have this. Perhaps you'd like to wrap it nicely and carry it home for me.'

Charmian's unfortunate misunderstanding in the bar led to a strain of rumour so potent that it reached Gerona. Even Luis' sister-in-law was considered an absolute tart because she left the washing up for an hour and read cheap love stories instead of going for the late afternoon constitutional in the park with her seven children. Gerona bourgeoisie had never seen anything like Charmian.

'There's a new sort of fly breeding on the coast,' said Luis' mother. 'Apparently it's been caused by an English pervert, a girl. I wonder if you know her.'

'I'm too tired for all this. I've been on my feet in that shop all day.'

'These flies could carry the plague, apparently. There'll be a disaster, you'll see.'

'Don't get pissed up,' said Norman.

'Why not?' Charmian replied. 'What is there to stay sober for?' He stared at her, and Jenny could see that a siesta was looming up. 'Oh no. Don't shut yourselves away, please! The kids can't take it.'

Norman put their drawing books on the terrace table and even left his paintbox. 'Won't be long,' he said and rushed Charmian into the bedroom.

There were the usual batterings and howlings outside the locked door. Offering them chocolate got them out on to the terrace, but only for a moment.

Norman came out after another moment and said, 'That was no good. I tried to keep them quiet but – No. It was no good.' A pause. 'She's drinking far too much. We'll let her sleep it off a bit and then go to the beach.'

The sand was too hot to walk barefoot. The only shade was under some rocks where everyone threw their rubbish. The water was murky.

'It's only because a lot of sand's been stirred up by so many people,' said Norman optimistically and ran in.

'He's so cold, Jenny. This afternoon he wouldn't even touch me.'

'But the siesta was his idea. He seemed desperate to – '

'Not at all. He just lay there unapproachable.'

'Perhaps the kids banging – '

'No, I was pleased they did. He's paying me back for Luis. He liked Luis. D'you know that? He blames me for the thing going wrong between them.'

Norman shook the water off him and sat down.

'If he's not married to Montserrat what does he do sexually?' Charmian asked. 'You can see he does something.'

'He has six women. All married.'

'And you're the seventh,' said Norman.

'No. I'm special.'

'I want some money,' said Charmian.

'Why?' He didn't look at her.

'I want a day on my own. Luis said I'd like Gerona.'

103

'Oh, did he?' said Jenny.

'Things will be better when James comes,' said Norman. 'He'll share the – ' He searched for a word instead of 'horror'; chose 'work'.

'I don't think James will share it. I've sent a telegram giving him a suggestion of how things are,' said Jenny.

'How much money have we got left?' Charmian asked.

'About 3,000 pesetas,' he said.

'Will it last till the end of August?'

'Not a hope.'

'Shall we send for more money, then?'

'No. When this money's finished, I'm going.' He stood up.

'But we've paid for the house, Norman,' she said.

'Why spend more money having a horrible time, Charmian?'

'It seems silly to go through so much and not get the benefit, Norman,' she said.

'Well, send for more money.'

'I haven't any more money.'

'I mean draw from the deposit account.' A pause. Something in her face made him ask, 'What's in the deposit account?'

'Nothing.'

Jenny supposed he felt dizzy, because he almost fell into a deck chair.

'You mean you've spent everything?'

'You know that.'

'I thought you were joking.'

'Joking?'

'Well, it's the sort of thing everyone says.' A pause. 'You've really spent all Laurence's money? I thought you were saying it out of bravado, to impress Jenny. When's his next salary?' he asked shakily.

'I don't know.'

He watched the waves flop in and out. 'What a day,' said Jenny.

'Dreadful,' said Norman. 'I've been through the whole range of my emotions this afternoon.'

'You've been very discreet about it,' Charmian said.

That evening there was a letter from Laurence saying he didn't want a divorce, he wanted her back. He loved her and would do everything he could to make the marriage work.

'It certainly makes me re-think things, Jenny. For the first time I'm in a strong position with Laurence. I can state my terms.'

'But a week ago you couldn't stand him.'

'I'm remembering the good things. God, Jenny, should I give up my marriage for Norman when he behaves like this? Could I live with him squabbling over 5p for a coffee? Being with him is no fun.'

'Haven't you noticed this before?'

'We've never been together all the time like this. He can't take it. At least Laurence enjoys life. Laurence has done a hell of a lot for me, you know. He's taught me how to think. Before I knew him I was nothing. I didn't know what I was doing.'

'Would Laurence be so enthusiastic if he knew Norman was here?'

'I'm going to write and tell him.'

'You're crazy.'

'I want to make a new start. You can't do that by being dishonest.'

Norman came on to the terrace and announced his evening plan. 'I'm going to the village. On my own.'

He went back inside.

Charmian looked worried.

'Say you're sorry,' said Jenny.

'Sorry! Let him say sorry to me.'

Out he came, wearing his new holiday blazer.

'Laurence has written to me.'

'How nice.' He withdrew behind his pipe and hid among the smoke. 'See you later, if you're still up. Have a good evening.' He looked at her, not really seeing her, and was gone.

Norman was angry with her. He didn't shout or hit out. He cut off, iced over, became polite. When he was angry with her he treated her the way he treated everybody most of the time.

'What are you going to do about James?'

James had written a letter in answer to Jenny's telegram which said that he was disappointed he wouldn't be coming out but when she'd chosen to go away with Charmian she must have forseen that the domestic set-up would be horrific. He concluded, 'You obviously prefer your self-destructive friends to me.'

'You've got to make a decision about him,' said Charmian. 'You've got to go back some time.'

'So have you.'

Norman had returned so outraged with Charmian that the only thing he could do was make love to her. It had been marvellous and reminded her that she didn't have with Laurence the sexual joy she had with Norman. 'If only I could have it all in one man, Jenny. What shall I do? I don't think I could ever leave Norman.'

Then Jenny had an idea. 'Why don't you ask Norman what he wants?' Looking back, Jenny's first feeling of unease about Norman had been when he had said, in London, 'Of course Charmian wouldn't be hurt if I left her.'

'Of course she would.'

'Never!' He didn't want anybody that involved. 'She'd go on just the same.'

Charmian had cut in, 'Of course I wouldn't be hurt, Jenny. I'd find someone else immediately.'

When they gave up the idea of trying to have a holiday they actually enjoyed themselves. They all ate together, went to bed at the same time, got up at Little Peter's chosen hour and felt relaxed. Laurence unexpectedly sent Charmian thirty pounds. She put it on the table. 'It's for all of us. It'll keep us for a few more days.' Her generosity made Norman and Jenny ashamed, and out slunk the hidden travellers' cheques.

'Lucky bags Norman!'

'Sweeties Norman!'

'Juice Norman!'

'When are we going to the beach, Norman? We haven't had any treats today.'

'But this is your treat,' he said magnanimously.

'What? Where?'

'Here. Being here in this garden.' He leapt on to the wall and did a jig, singing, 'Lucky bags, lucky lollies, ice cream, suck lollies. Doughnuts, juice, I want drawing books and biscuits and sweeties too.'

The kids watched him, open-mouthed. He'd gone mad at last.

They had their curlers in and face packs on. Jenny was plucking her eyebrows and Charmian polishing her nails. A lot of grooming suddenly – but then Luis was coming. Norman swept the floor. Charmian held out a piece of cotton wool. 'Wet it for me, Norman, and bring the brandy.'

A rebellious Cinders put down his broom. 'Oh, Charmian, I've been on my feet all day.'

The moment she started on the hard stuff they'd be taken back into her past to hear about her men and how they'd adored her. It was all true, of course. At one time it used to torment Norman, but now he said, 'We're off. Reminiscence time. What's it tonight? The man in Zurich? No, on second thoughts let's have the near rape in New York. I need a laugh.'

'Laurence is funny,' she said. 'Such a sense of humour. And generous. Before he left for Africa he said, Have you any money? I said I hadn't, thinking he was going to take the little I had. Well, here you are, he said, and he emptied his wallet. Have the lot. I won't need it.'

'Norman, feel guilty immediately,' Jenny said.

'I'm enjoying it. These stories get better every time

I hear them. The characters are becoming old friends.'

Then Charmian said something that really surprised them, and she wasn't even drunk. In the middle of the floor, covered as it was with various baby goos and messes, a pile of used disposable napkins staring at her from the open lavatory door, she said, 'I'd like another baby. Yes, I would.'

'Not by me, you won't,' said Norman immediately. 'You're surrounded by all this,' he waved his hand, 'and you can't cope with any of it. Then just when things might at last get a bit better because they're growing up, you suggest putting yourself back in again. That's crazy, Charmian.'

Out came a letter. 'Laurence says maybe the answer for us is another child. Me and him he means.' She giggled.

'I've never heard anything so ridiculous. Well, I won't help you through it.'

'Laurence says' – Laurence, like a ghost, was walking through the conversation again – 'He wants to make me happy. Yes, I'd like a child. I'd like to give it everything. Lots of time and care.'

'I'd concentrate on giving the ones you've already got time and care,' said Norman.

There was a whipping wind blowing stinging sand into their eyes and making the sheets on the line crack like gunfire. Glasses broke. They saved the wine.

'Let's go inside,' said Charmian, as she was blown against the door. Luis looked at the mountains and laughed. The whole countryside was howling.

The children clustered round Luis. He'd given them rides on a blanket, drawn pictures, dressed them up as pirates, sung songs. He'd made a log fire, and its brightness transformed the room. Charmian had just dazzled them with a splendid meal, and Luis said how impressed he was.

'She can cook a feast for twenty people,' said Norman. 'But she has trouble preparing an ordinary breakfast or changing a napkin.'

'How's your work going?' Charmian asked. 'I'd like to come and see the house.'

He was no longer decorating the house outside Barcelona, he said, as the marriage was off. 'She changed her mind. It was a terrible thing. All the relatives trooped into the house and pleaded with her and the fiancé was white, like this.' He slapped the wall. 'I thought he would fall to the ground. This, all in front of us, the workmen. The presents have gone back and the house will be closed and sold.'

'What do you think of marriage?' Charmian asked.

'It's all right. For other people.'

'He's a cool one. I love his eyes. They're so hot.' She stared at him and went on staring, and because of the positions they were sitting in no one could shift forward and block her gaze.

Luis stared back at first, then looked away. It was the sort of thing that would have Norman on the kip, face to wall, speechless. No one could move. Then Jenny got up, walked round the table, stood in front of Luis and suggested a walk if the wind dropped.

Norman, all normality and composure, asked,

'Do you enjoy working in the shop, Luis?'

After coffee there was a demonstration of helplessness – Charmian putting her kids to bed. Luis watched it for twenty minutes and then did it for her. They stood together in the dark of the children's room.

'What's this? Telling him about her problems, is she?' Jenny's eyes were glowing like a cat's. It was time for her to get Luis out of the house altogether. 'Shall we go to the village?' she asked him.

'Let's see how the weather is.' He went on to the terrace.

Charmian went after him and gave him a brandy. 'Laurence doesn't care, you see. Not even about his children, Luis.'

Jenny sat beside him, although she'd heard the problems a hundred times.

'He beats Little Peter for nothing. Yes, for nothing.'

Jenny tried to speak, but Charmian didn't want to listen. 'What can I do, Luis?'

Jenny got up and went inside. Norman was calmly reading. 'Will you please stop Charmian.'

He knew what she meant and was on the terrace in a flash saying something about going to sleep. He and Charmian to bed was what he meant. Luis and Charmian didn't listen.

Luis was saying she should get help for the children.

'Psychiatric help?'

'Domestic help. You would then be free to do some work.'

'A job! That's a good idea. But what? What could I do?'

'What do you want to do?'

They went through a hundred possibilities.

He snapped his fingers. 'Research!'

Research! She was thrilled. Now her life wouldn't be wasted, he said. She wouldn't be resentful about cleaning lavatories and sweeping floors, and she'd actually enjoy the time spent with the children.

Charmian sorted out, he stood up.

Wait! Research into what, she wanted to know.

Norman sighed loudly. Charmian had Luis where she wanted him – involved and helping her. Next step? The bed. Right under their noses, she'd do it. Another brandy was pressed into Luis' hand.

'Laurence must help you,' said Luis. 'He'll be able to get you something technical.'

Then she made the big mistake – she got drunk. Between one brandy and the next it happened, and she lolled, eyes scarlet, over the side of her chair.

He got up. 'Right, Jenny! A walk.'

'No,' he said later. 'I do not fancy her.'

'You said she was beautiful.'

'I said she's not ugly.'

'You spend a lot of time with her.'

'For the children I do it. If I was her husband I would throw her through the window. But I like her.' He laughed. 'Tonight she's like something preserved in alcohol. Only her eyes are alive.'

X

The first meeting of the association of Catalan artists was held in Olot, a village north of Gerona. Luis sat at the top of the table and proposed plans to protect Catalan style, the Catalan language, from the plebeian influence of the rest of Spain. Elsewhere in the province a group of people were discussing plans to protect Catalan money, which the rest of Spain was far more concerned about. Luis had already approached several international artists to become 'friends of Catalonia'. People listened to him, and he wasn't altogether relying on optimism when he said, 'In a month I will be on the Mayor's payroll.'

It was after the speeches that the 'House of Flies' crept into the conversation.

'The tourists are a lot of skunks generally,' said Pedro Picolivas, the sculptor. 'They can't hold their booze. The women can't keep their drawers on. Especially the English. Of course it's not unusual for them to have their streets swilling with vomit. They're so ugly – though in the last few years the girls have improved.'

'Their clothes have improved,' said Montserrat. 'But they're still the same.'

'No, I speak from experience,' said Pedro. 'The girls are quite lovely. But the English have no style. The way they live! Like pigs. Why, right now, just along the coast, there's a household of pigs.'

'D'you mean the lesbian brothel?' asked Luis.

'It isn't a brothel.' said Pedro. 'The women are lesbians, yes. Two of them, about thirty – they look fifty. They're alcoholic. They also fuck with the man they've got there who's like Cinderella. He does all the shopping, the cleaning. He waits on them hand and foot.'

Luis felt shaky. 'Where is this?'

'San Pedro Pescador. But they're certainly not whores. They're shit eaters.'

'I've heard about them,' said a woman. 'They have nine children, all by Cinderella. They eat shit too.'

Luis nearly fell under the table.

The hostess laughed. 'They sound German.'

'They're English,' said Pedro. 'The really wild one goes around wearing nothing but a thin blouse and saying, "I fuck like a lion". It hasn't got her any partners so far.'

'Mother of God.' Luis gripped the table.

'Are you all right, friend? You look pale.'

'It's the heat.'

'But it's cool,' said Montserrat.

'How do you know this family?' Luis asked feebly.

'My cleaning woman is the cousin of their cleaning woman, and has she a story to tell! Hostia! She says they worship shit. The pretty girl makes Cinderella lie down. Then she sits – '

'I cannot tolerate this talk,' said Luis.

'Squeamish!'

'That's not like you, Luis.'

114

'The cleaning woman says every day the house is covered in shit, piss and blood, because the women don't bother to wear protections and they have periods all the time.'

'What are they doing there, I wonder?' asked Montserrat.

'Having an orgy. My friend Ramiro is forming a sightseeing group to go to San Pedro at the weekend. We'll have to go soon before the public health is called in. They are a health hazard to the village, and the people are up in arms.'

'Yes, let's go,' cried Montserrat. 'We'll take binoculars and Dettol. It'll be fun.'

'Apparently their filth has produced a new strain of household fly.'

'I'm going to faint,' Luis murmured.

Jenny was delighted by Luis' unexpected night-time visit and made room for him in her bed.

'No, no! You must leave immediately. There's going to be a scandal. I tell you, there has been nothing like it on the Costa Brava.'

'How can we? The children are all asleep. Come on. Get into bed.'

He realised that dragging five children and three adults from their beds in the middle of the night to begin an unprepared journey to London was hardly sensible, so he gave himself up to a night of pleasure with the girl who gave him most, though he could not have said why.

They overslept, and the sun was high and the children disorderly when Luis appeared on the terrace. Charmian was unusually fresh and wanted action.

'I want an excursion. I want to look at some Spaniards. I want to visit churches. I haven't seen a thing since I got here.'

Luis took Norman to one side. 'The local people are talking.'

'Rubbish. What about? They seem perfectly friendly.'

'About the flies and Little Peter.'

'They seem perfectly relaxed to me. Anyway, children do make a mess!' He sucked on his pipe and got the push-chair ready for the market.

'I seriously think you should return to London.'

'We've paid till the end of the month and we'll stay. If the Spanish are worried about hygiene I suggest they concentrate on their beaches.'

Jenny found a handful of lottery tickets in Luis' pocket.

'The fat lottery. The tourist lottery. What are these?'

'My future.'

He wouldn't come to the beach no matter how they pleaded with him. He wouldn't even sit outside. He took Charmian into her bedroom and tried to get into her head the Spanish conception of housework and child rearing. The only thing he succeeded in was making Jenny jealous.

'There are always flies in summer,' said Charmian.

He looked at two flies fornicating in a smear of slime on her sheet. 'No, this is something different. Little Peter must wear pants in public.'

'I know the Spanish are mad about bleach, and I know all about these bourgeois phobias you're so keen on, but frankly I haven't seen much for me to be keen on. It seems to me your earlier promise has been dissipated in house painting and the trinket trade.'

Stung, he said, 'I have, as a matter of fact, formed a Catalan association. They have nominated me their leader. I will have a very telling effect on the future of this province, don't doubt me. Tomorrow will decide whether or not my position is official.'

'What happens tomorrow?'

'There is a very important meeting which I have organised. The mayor will be there.'

'Where?'

'At a large gallery,' he admitted, sulkily.

'Does it have a name?'

'Why shouldn't it?' And he told her. 'You obviously don't believe me.'

'There's always so much in the air, but nothing ever seems to happen.' She still hadn't got over his domestic advice. 'These schemes for rescuing Spain. They're always a bit flyblown.'

'We shall see. Anyway, if I can rid Spain of the polluting effect of the filthy foreigners, my schemes will not be for nothing.'

She laughed. 'Oh, shut up and have a drink.' She poured him a brandy.

'Tomorrow I shall be making the speeches. There will be over two hundred guests. I have always worked like a pig. For what? Tomorrow is my big chance. I

will be on the payroll. Then I will be liberated from –
well, liberated.'

Jenny came into the bedroom.

'Sssh!' he signalled to Charmian, but she said, 'When
will this – '

He shook his head violently.

Angrily Jenny picked up a wine bottle and went out
with it.

Intrigued, Charmian moved closer and poured him
an enormous brandy. Why was it *she* could know, but
Jenny couldn't? She saw him looking at her naked left
breast. Then she understood. 'Where is this gallery?'
she asked softly.

'Gerona,' he whispered. 'Keep it secret.'

She nodded. 'But of course.'

He stayed inside until it was dark. He'd told Jenny
and Norman he had a business trip to Tarragona the
next day.

As he was leaving, Charmian rushed up and whispered, 'Tomorrow then.' Her eyes were excited.

He wondered what she could possibly mean. Was she
wishing him luck? He put it down to a misunderstanding in the language.

She was sure it was an invitation. In the past men had
used roundabout schemes to get her to bed but nothing
quite like this. What had mayors and payrolls got to do
with it? Luis was colourful. 'Tomorrow is the big day,'
he'd said over and over. Telling me, she thought, as
she stole 1,000 pesetas from Norman's pocket.

She was wearing her seducer's outfit – very short

transparent dress and no bra. In the taxi she took off
her knickers. She'd already put down a lot of drink.
It hadn't been easy to convince Norman that she'd
appreciate Gaudi architecture in Barcelona better if
she went alone. And although she wanted to get one
up on Jenny, she felt guilty.

She stopped outside Gerona and had a large drink
to build up her confidence. Then she thought how
sexily he'd looked at her body, how subtle he'd been
arranging the rendezvous.

'There's no flies on him,' she muttered and got back
in the taxi.

Luis' big chance was not a political meeting, even a
cultural one, but a not uncommon occasion on which a
respectable citizen received an award for services to art.
The respectable citizen was Montserrat, and Luis was
in charge of arranging the platform. He'd not spared
her money. Flowers and leaves were twined artistically
between her water colours. Some said his flower
arrangement showed more talent than what it was
decorating. There was an expanse of food and wine
along one side of the room; a three-piece group played
mediaeval music. He'd arranged chairs for the forty
guests in the centre of the gallery. He and the mayor
would preside on the platform, which was reached by
a door each side. One led to the cloakroom, the other
to the street. Montserrat's family, his mother, his sister
and two journalists sat in the front row, Pedro and the
artists of Gerona behind.

Luis made a long speech in which he outlined publicly his plans for his beloved province. He'd managed to squeeze enough money from the platform fund to buy a new suit. His shoes though were still full of holes. After the applause the mayor made a short speech in praise of Luis' dedication.

Luis stood up again. He'd never seen his mother look so happy.

'And now our local painter, our great painter, Montserrat Garcia Ortega.'

He waved his arm in the cloakroom direction and waited for her to appear. The pipe band started playing. But behind him, the door to the street was flung open and Charmian, fresh from a booster dose of alcohol in the bar next door, swayed in. Wine soaked her see-through dress. Her eyes were glazed. She wouldn't have been able to see the audience anyway. They were too far back, behind the pillars. She saw Luis though and stumbled towards him, arms outstretched.

In San Pedro, two hours before, Norman had said, 'As Miss Sloppychops has gone sightseeing, let's take advantage and go to the market in Gerona. Luis says its very cheap.'

Charmian threw her arms around Luis as Montserrat appeared from the cloakroom. The fiancée still had her official smile quivering at the corners of her mouth as she sank to the floor. Luis' mother screamed and fell forward.

'It's the woman from the house of flies,' shouted Pedro.

Some people left in panic. The mayor was hustled out. Luis' sister was hysterical. An ambulance was

120

called for Montserrat. 'Tilt her up. No, lie her down. It's her heart.'

'I thought it was going to be just you and me,' Charmian told Luis. But being a girl who could take chaos in her stride she turned to the fragmented audience and started talking to them.

Pedro was licking his lips. He'd never seen a whore in an art gallery before. Antonio helped revive the fallen. 'There goes Luis' chance of being mayor.'

Luis' mother was escorted into the street. She thought Charmian was Jenny. Although she'd hated Jenny for years, she never had a clear idea what she looked like.

Charmian, a drink in each hand, the journalists hungrily around her, believed she was a wild success. 'I find the Spanish men so friendly.'

Jenny and Norman trundled the pushchair up the narrow street. The kids were bellowing for ice lollies.

'Good God!' said Norman. 'Look at that group. Half of them are laughing, the others crying. Look at that old woman, with her head in her hands. It's real chaos.' He chuckled. 'All it lacks is Charmian.'

121

XI

There was a violent sound in the bedroom. Jenny thought Norman was beating Charmian, but he was killing flies with a rolled up newspaper.

Charmian was sitting up in bed, confident. Norman was always being reminded how other men fancied her – she was quite sure that now he'd make some statement about their future, the one she wanted to hear. 'Do you think Luis will still come to see Jenny?'

'He said he would, but disappointment's always been a big part of their affair,' said Norman.

'He's mysterious.'

'He's got *joie de vivre*,' said Norman. 'I wish I had.'

Jenny went outside and heard Charmian say, 'I've never seen Jenny so happy. He fills her up with life.'

'I can't imagine him marrying her or even keeping her,' said Norman.

Jenny walked down to the gate and heard her say, 'We spend a lot of time talking about Jenny and Luis. What about us, Norman?'

Charmian was sitting on the terrace. She seemed to have shrunk; the inside of her had caved in. But she was not a weeper, Charmian. She lit a cigarette and looked at her nails.

'God, they're long. They're horrible, aren't they, Jenny? It's the way they do them at the hairdressers. Real Golders Green nails. Those days are over. I've no money left. Maybe I'll dye my hair myself. Black, perhaps.'

'Where's Norman?'

'Gone off to do some sketches. I've asked him outright about our future, and he says he won't marry me.'

'I'm sorry. Maybe it's these weeks in Spain that have changed his mind.'

'No. He says he's never had any intention of marrying me. He says I'm too much for him. He needs someone easier. He doesn't want the responsibility . . . We've never discussed our affair. I'd always thought Laurence stopped us living together. Now I know Laurence isn't a rival but a necessary part of our scene. Laurence pays the bills, you see, and supports the children. He stops the question of future.' One tear dropped down her cheek.

'But Laurence would give you a generous settlement.'

'Norman knows that. I'm just a stage in his life. I always thought I dominated him. I've realised he only allows what he wants to come into the affair.'

'What will you do now?'

'Leave him. He'll marry some seventeen-year-old who he can dominate completely.'

Little Peter lunged on to the terrace and got hold of her. 'The only man in my life,' she said.

'You have pissed about, Charmian. He's been a ringer for Cinderella most of the time. Show him you can change.'

'I'm what he wants, for godsake. He forces me into this role. I don't want it.'

'Will he go on seeing you?'

'Of course. He's quite prepared for our affair to continue in the way it always has. No commitments, no responsibility. But the joy's gone out of it. It's all drawn-together brows and silences now. Norman can't stand my life. It's the last thing I expected. I feel very – I feel terrible.'

'Did you really want him?'

'Of course. Anyway, let's forget it.' She looked at her nails again. 'This doing nothing is very depleting. I should have something to do. Luis is right. I should get a job.'

The note enclosed with the engagement ring demanded the return of the shop keys. He was no longer welcome there, or at Montserrat's family house.

The doctor had given his mother a sedative, but she was still lively. 'You must get her back. Your whole future is with that spinster. Don't throw your life into a slop pail because of that English girl.'

'I thought you'd be pleased,' said Luis. 'After all you hate Montserrat.'

'You can't live without that money.'

'You could have a marriage contract that entitled you to fifty per cent of everything,' said his brother. 'You could still have had foreign whores. On the side. You've to think of your family. You can't just throw a fortune away.'

'You must pursue her,' said his sister. 'You must beg

her to marry you. You must sit on her step crying all night. For me and my children you must do that. My husband is so disgusted he threatens to abandon us. You have soiled his name.'

But it was the sight of the bleached and starched squinting little girls that decided him. He thought of Jenny's children, their wildness and pleasure. He missed them.

He fanned his face. 'I think Gerona's too hot for me in more ways than one.'

He packed a huge case containing fly spray, disinfectant, fly papers, bleach. Everyone thought he was mad. Antonio said, 'Now he can no longer be mayor, he's going to be a travelling salesman.'

Having decided she was going to have a new life, Charmian couldn't wait to leave. They packed and were getting the night train to Paris. Jenny dithered between waiting for Luis, going back to James or just going back. Her life was as uncertain as Charmian's.

As they got into the taxi, Charmian said, 'When we next meet, our lives will be very different, Jenny.'

'I doubt it,' said Norman.

'What do you mean?' she asked sharply.

'People don't change. She'll be back with James in under a week and we'll go on as usual.' He smiled.

'You speak for yourself.' She was furious.

He was right of course. In the end she couldn't even get a job. He wouldn't let her, as he liked their siestas too much.

'If Luis does come, don't let him keep things too

125

clean,' said Norman. 'Now we've gone you could end up with a bourgeois house.' He picked up his folio of sketches – about thirty views of the area. 'The village,' he said. 'The coast. The mountains. The countryside. Our house. San Pedro. Never again.'

'Poor Norman. He's had the worst time,' said Jenny. Norman didn't disagree.

Charmian said, 'We've had a lot of laughs.'

'You've had a lot of laughs,' he said. 'It's been a working holiday for me. I've got nothing out of it.' He closed the folio.

'Oh, leave them for godsake,' said Charmian. 'We've got enough rubbish to carry.'

The sketches had been done to stop him going mad. They were just something to do between the shopping and the cooking, and he nearly did leave them behind.

In London, people looking at them said, 'Spain has such tranquillity, such excitement. It must be a marvellous place to enjoy oneself.'

He sold the pictures for over two thousand pounds.

Also by Patrice Chaplin

NIGHT FISHING
An Urban Tale

Night Fishing is about sons who go wrong, mothers who don't see trouble until it's too late and fathers who aren't there. At the heart of this moving and all-too-familiar terror is Jaimie, a sweet boy, 'beautiful with a radiance', who finds the ultimate sweetness in street drugs. His mother is Janice, a documentary filmmaker who thinks she has her finger on the pulse; his father, a rich and famous man who sees the world through his camera lens; his friends, the teenagers who roam the back streets of London and tell their mothers they're just going night fishing.

With compassion and wit, the author of *Albany Park* and *Having it Away* has written a pithy, hard-hitting urban tragedy – a story for our times.

INTO THE DARKNESS LAUGHING
The Story of Modigliani's Last Mistress, Jeanne Hébuterne

In the years of the First World War, somewhere in Montparnasse, a young artist, Jeanne Hébuterne, met the Italian painter Amedeo Modigliani. She was a young girl with a farouche beauty and a talent recognised by Foujita and Severini. He was in his thirties, unstable, penniless, unrecognised. From 1917 they lived together in Modigliani's studio. Jeanne posing for him continually, as he, increasingly embittered, found escape in drink. By the freezing January of 1920 Modigliani's health had failed. For a week he lay dying of tubercular meningitis with only Jeanne beside him. Too late, they were found by the Chilean painter Ortiz de Zárate. Modigliani died in the Charity Hospital. The following day Jeanne, nine months pregnant, fell to her death from a fifth floor window.

For years speculation has surrounded Jeanne Hébuterne. Now, in an extraordinary chain of coincidences, Patrice Chaplin has unearthed letters, photographs and drawings not previously seen. Carefully researched and passionately written, this compelling book will at last cast a full light on the short life and tragic death of Jeanne Hébuterne.